SWEET TIME IN SECONDS

A SWEET COVE, MASSACHUSETTS COZY
MYSTERY BOOK 11

J. A. WHITING

To hear about new books and book sales, please sign up for my mailing list at:

www.jawhitingbooks.com

❀ Created with Vellum

For my family with love

CONTENTS

1

The early June sky was a clear, deep blue and the sun's rays sparkled off the ocean. The white foam of the waves glittered like thousands of little diamonds as the water crashed against the white sand beach causing Angie and Ellie Roseland's shrieks and laughter to fill the air.

On the spur of the moment and because the day was so beautiful, Ellie suggested they take the first jump of the season into the freezing ocean and when the two sisters stepped their feet into the water, they almost backed out as their toes and ankles went numb from the cold.

"No turning back now," Ellie called as a big wave rose up and headed towards them. Crashing into their legs and sending spray over their heads, the wave hit the two young women as they rushed head-long into the ocean and dove under the water. When they bobbed back to the surface, Angie and Ellie scrambled to their feet and ran for the shore, stumbling in the waves and screaming from the shock of the cold.

"This was a crazy idea," Angie said shivering, but exhilarated as she reached down for the towel she'd left on the sand and wrapped it around herself.

"It's not the earliest we've ever been in, but I think it's the coldest the water has been for our first dip of the year." Ellie used her towel to wring out her long, blond hair.

The young women sat in the sand to warm themselves by soaking up the golden rays of the sun and Angie's engagement ring sparkled in the light. Every time she looked down to see the ring on her finger, her heart swelled with love for Josh Williams, her new fiancé.

"Wait until Jenna and Courtney hear we went in." Angie smiled watching three more people at the water's edge getting ready for a plunge.

Angie's twin sister, Jenna, and Tom were newly-married and had taken a long weekend away to Maine to stay in an historic inn in a pretty town on the coast. The youngest Roseland sister, Courtney, was on a bike ride with her English boyfriend, Rufus.

Ellie stood up and reached into her tote bag for her phone. "Let's take a picture to send everyone as proof of what we just did."

Angie put her arm around her sister's shoulders and they stood with their backs to the sea smiling for the camera with their hair and swimsuits dripping wet. Ellie texted the photo to their two sisters and to the family friend, Mr. Finch.

Walking up the sidewalk from the beach to their Victorian mansion home, Angie and Ellie discussed the upcoming week. "The bed and breakfast is almost sold out this week and we have tons of summer reservations. The season seems to be kicking into full gear earlier than usual."

Angie agreed. "The bake shop has been bustling. Lots of tourists stopping in, more than I've ever had at this time of year."

Passing Jenna and Tom's house, Ellie admired the flowers in the front bed. "Look how nice these are filling in. I need to water the flowerpots tonight."

Angie slipped her sunglasses on. "It's been hot. The heat is kicking in early this summer, too."

When they approached the house, they saw Mr. Finch and their two cats, Euclid, a huge orange

Maine Coon, and Circe, a sweet black cat with a little patch of white at her chest, sitting on the big front porch watching the people stroll by. Finch waved and the cats trilled as Angie and Ellie climbed the steps to the porch.

"We saw your photograph," Finch told them. "It must have been delightful."

"You can join us next time, Mr. Finch." Angie gave the man a big smile and touched his arm with her icy hand. "It's very refreshing."

Finch adjusted his eyeglasses and chuckled. "I must say I do prefer warm water, Miss Angie. I'll leave the ice cold ocean to you." Mr. Victor Finch, a spry, older man who walked with a cane, met the four Roseland sisters a year ago and was now an adopted member of their family.

The girls went inside to shower and change and Finch and the cats headed to the kitchen so the man could put the tea kettle on. When Angie and Ellie finished changing and came into the room, they sat at the table with Mr. Finch, sipped their hot teas, and each had a slice of cinnamon crumb cake.

"Jenna and Tom will be back tomorrow," Finch noted. "I miss them even though they've only been gone for three days."

"I know. I do, too." Ellie added a dollop of whipped cream to her cake.

When Angie grinned, the corners of her blue eyes crinkled a little. "They aren't allowed to have any more vacations without us."

"The funny thing is," Finch said, "Tom and Jenna would probably be happy to agree to that."

Euclid and Circe trilled from their perch on top of the refrigerator, leapt down, and tore out of the room for the front foyer.

"What's up with them?" Ellie watched the two furry whirlwinds rush from the kitchen.

They heard the front door open and Jenna's voice call out. "Where is everyone? Anyone home?"

"They're back?" Finch's face beamed with delight.

Jenna and Tom walked into the kitchen just as Angie, Ellie, and Mr. Finch stood up to go and greet them.

"We came back a little early," Tom announced with a smile. "Turns out, there's no place like home."

Jenna's long brown hair slid over her shoulders as she hugged the three people standing before her. "We know it's silly, but we missed home so we came back."

Everyone took seats at the table, tea was poured,

and the cake was sliced for the two surprise arrivals. Chatter moved from the short trip Tom and Jenna had taken and what they'd done and seen to their recent wedding festivities, Angie's engagement, and Ellie and Angie's jump in the freezing ocean.

"It certainly is a busy household." Finch raised his teacup and happily sipped.

"What's cookin'?" Carrying her bicycle helmet, the youngest Roseland came in through the back door dressed in shorts and a colorful short-sleeved biking shirt. Her honey blond hair was pulled up in a high ponytail. "When did you two get back?" Courtney asked.

"Just a few minutes ago," Jenna told her sister.

"We didn't want to miss out on anything so we decided to come home." Tom kidded as he gave Courtney a hug. "Where's Rufus?"

"He went home to change. He'll be back for dinner."

"Speaking of which." Ellie stood up. "I'm going to make a tomato pie and there are chicken kebobs for the grill. Let's eat outside on the patio tonight. It's going to be a beautiful evening."

Courtney put her bike helmet on the floor near the back door and when she turned around, she lifted both arms so the family could see the red, raw scrapes running from her wrists to her elbows. "I had a little accident."

Ellie's eyes were as wide as saucers and the others let out gasps of surprise.

Angie hurried to her sister's side and clucked over the injuries firing questions at her about the accident. "What happened? We need to clean the cuts so they don't get infected. Did you hit your head? Are you okay? Do you feel dizzy? Why don't you sit down?"

Courtney couldn't help but chuckle. "I'm okay, sis. It was just a spill."

Angie maneuvered her sister to a chair. "Sit for a minute and rest. I'll get a face cloth."

"What caused the tumble, Miss Courtney?" Finch looked over the long scrapes on her arms.

"We were riding on the rail trail and there was a sandy spot. My front tire went deep into the sand and the bike wobbled and I went over the handlebars."

Ellie put her hand over her mouth. "Did you hit your head?"

"My arms took the impact of most of the fall." Courtney used her index finger to lift her lip a little. "I broke my tooth." A small piece of a premolar had broken off.

7

"Does it hurt?" Jenna asked, standing up to get a closer look at the tooth.

"Not bad. A little sensitive."

"Call your dentist," Tom suggested. "Get in to have it fixed before more of it breaks off."

"Way ahead of you." Courtney smiled. "I called from the trail. I have an appointment bright and early tomorrow morning." Her eyes clouded and her smile faded when she whispered, "I hate the dentist." Turning to Angie, she asked, "I know I'm being a baby and should go by myself, but will you come with me?"

"Of course." As Angie walked to the sink with paper towels and a wash cloth, a shiver of unease ran through her body, and not knowing what caused the uncomfortable sensation, she tried to brush it off by focusing on her sister's injuries.

Courtney was always anxious about visiting the dentist so she often brought Angie along for moral support. Angie was born only a few minutes before her twin, Jenna, yet the family considered her the oldest sibling and she took the designation to heart, always looking out for everyone and making sure things were all right. Sometimes, minutes ... and seconds ... could make a world of difference.

"Here's what you need to use to clean the

8

scrapes." Angie waved her sister over and Courtney stood and went to the sink, turned on the water, and took care of her torn up skin.

"Good thing you had your helmet on." Angie leaned against the counter absent-mindedly watching Courtney wash her cuts. Something worrisome was bouncing around in the air and she wondered if Courtney could feel it, too.

Ever since moving to the seaside town of Sweet Cove, the Roseland sisters had been developing some interesting skills. Angie had the unique ability to put intention into what she baked. She could make people feel happy or feel compelled to tell the truth about something. Once, her intention backfired when preparing some muffins and Mr. Finch fell in love with her for a few hours. Angie was a lot more careful with her baking after that experience.

Ellie, although not happy about it and would only use it in an emergency, had the skill of telekinesis ... which had come in handy more than once.

Jenna could see or sense ghosts and Courtney....

Courtney leaned close to Angie. "I feel something weird on the air. It's making me anxious and it has nothing to do with having the dentist work on my tooth. I've felt it since I fell off the bike." When

9

she shifted her eyes away from her scrapes to Angie's face, she didn't need to ask the question that was on her mind. "You feel it, too, huh?"

Angie let out a sigh and she and Courtney looked across the room to Mr. Finch who sat at the table listening to Tom and Jenna talk about their long weekend away. He lifted his eyes to Courtney and Angie and both of his eyebrows raised a little as he gave them the slightest of nods.

Mr. Finch felt the very same thing.

From the top of the refrigerator, Euclid let out a loud, howling screech that made everyone in the kitchen jump.

"Here we go again," Courtney said to Angie.

2

Angie sat in the dentist's waiting room reading a book on her phone while Courtney jiggled her leg, fiddled with a few strands of her hair, and let her eyes flick about the room like a crazy person. Her cheeks were flushed pink. She let out a long sigh. "I can't stand waiting in the dentist's office. It makes me so nervous."

Angie glanced at her sister's jumpy leg twitching away. "Yeah, I know what you mean."

"Sorry." Courtney knew her jiggling distracted Angie, but it was hard to keep it from happening when she was so nervous. She consciously stopped her leg from moving, but after a few seconds of inattention, the limb began its rhythmic jerking all over again.

Unable to keep reading, Angie closed the app on her phone and placed it in her lap deciding she'd wait to continue with her book until her sister was called by the dental assistant and led away to the examination room.

The receptionist looked over at the Roselands with an apologetic expression. "I don't know what's keeping them. Maybe they're having car trouble."

The husband and wife dentists worked together in the practice in the center of Sweet Cove. Courtney, who had the earliest appointment of the day, had been waiting for over forty-five minutes.

The receptionist added, "I called the house *and* their cell phones, but no one is answering. This never happens. I'm so sorry to keep you waiting."

An icy rush sped through Angie's veins and she shifted nervously in her seat. She'd been on edge ever since she and Courtney had arrived at the office.

"Maybe they'll show up in a minute." Courtney gave a little smile to the woman at the desk. In reality, she hoped the two dentists never showed up so that she could run home to escape from the dental work.

"Other than worrying about your tooth, how do you feel?" Angie asked.

"I'm just a jumble of worry. I don't know if it's the

same feeling as yesterday or I'm just freaked out about being here." Courtney rolled her eyes. "Or both."

"Courtney," the receptionist spoke from the desk. "Can I reschedule you for tomorrow? I don't think it's worth you waiting any longer."

Courtney hurried over. "Oh, sure. I don't mind." Her voice was practically joyful.

After making the appointment, the sisters stepped out of the office onto the brick sidewalk into the bright, June sunshine and strolled through the pretty town of shops and restaurants. It was still early in the morning and most places hadn't yet opened. Trees lined the streets and their leafy branches provided cooling shade over the walkways.

"I still feel weird," Courtney said. "Even though I'm out of there."

"How do you feel?" Angie asked. "Like what?"

"Jumpy, nervous. Something's wrong, but I don't know what it is." Courtney ran her hand over her arm to rid her skin of the goosebumps that had formed.

"I feel the same. It's getting more intense." Angie stopped walking and pointed to the bench at the edge of the sidewalk. "Let's sit for a little while, put our heads together, see if we can figure out what the cause of the tension is."

When they were settled, Courtney said, "It started for me after I fell off the bike."

"Right away? Think back."

Courtney took in some deep breaths while she thought about the crash. "It started when I felt my tooth, when I realized I'd broken it."

Angie looked sideways at her sister. "It started for me when you told us you broke your tooth."

They held one another's eyes for several seconds as Courtney moved her hand to her cheek.

Angie said softly, "Dr. Chase and Dr. Streeter are over an hour late."

"The receptionist told us the dentists are never late." Courtney's voice sounded tight. "She called their phones and no one answered."

Angie felt the blood run out of her head. "It's them, isn't it?" she whispered.

Courtney's cheeks had lost their color. "What should we do? We know where they live. Should we walk over there?"

The two dentists lived on the edge of town, about two miles away, on ten acres of land in a big, beautiful, twenty-room manor house. The Roselands had been to the house last year as one of the stops on the town-wide house and garden tour and discovered that their dentists now owned the place.

"If we walk, it would take about thirty minutes to get there." Angie checked the time. "Let's call Jenna and tell her what's going on. She can pick us up and drive over. I'll text Louisa at the bake shop and tell her I'll be in a little later than expected."

Jenna arrived and Angie and Courtney brought her up to speed as they drove the distance from town passing by meadows, marshes, and residential neighborhoods and crossing over a small bridge that spanned an inlet river. They turned onto the shady lane, headed for the house, and pulled to a stop at the curb. When they got out of the car, a trickle of sweat showed at Courtney's temple as she took her Angie's arm. "I'm feeling more anxious than I did before."

"Yeah," was all Angie could manage to say. Her heart pounded like a hammer was hitting her chest and her palms were wet and clammy.

Part of the manor house could be seen set back from the road at the end of a long driveway. The three young women stood at the curb staring down to the house. There was a sporty, blue vehicle parked in front of the detached three-car garage to the right of the home.

The neighbors' houses couldn't be seen through the thick growth of trees on both sides of the property. No one was around. All they could hear were birds singing and the rustling of leaves high in the trees.

"Should we go up to the house?" Jenna asked, peering down the driveway.

"Do you think we should go knock?" Courtney's voice trembled a little.

Angie hesitated for a moment as she kept her eyes on the house. There was a strange scent on the air. "Do you smell something?"

Jenna said slowly, "Maybe."

Courtney gave her sisters a strange look and the pitch of her voice sounded higher than usual. "What do you smell? I don't smell anything."

"I don't know what it is," Angie said, but she could detect a very distinct odor similar to what she'd experienced when she and Courtney found Mr. Finch's miserable brother stabbed to death in the candy shop a year ago.

"It smells like blood." Jenna shoved her hands into the pockets of her light windbreaker.

"What should we do?" Courtney asked warily.

Angie reached into her back pocket and took out her phone. "I'm going to call Chief Martin."

A look of relief mixed with dread passed over Courtney's face and she sagged down to sit on the curb to wait. "Good."

⁓

IT SEEMED LIKE FOREVER, but in reality, it only took about ten minutes for Chief Martin to pull to the side of the road just a little past where the girls were waiting.

The chief, a tall, stocky man in his fifties, emerged from the vehicle and walked towards the Roselands. He'd known the girls since they were little when they came to town in the summers to visit their grandmother. Their nana had special skills, too, and sometimes she worked closely with the police to assist on difficult cases. Chief Martin was happy to now have the same kind of help from her granddaughters.

"So." The chief greeted the three Roselands and glanced down the driveway. "You have some concerns?"

"We do." Angie repeated the worries she'd shared with the chief over the phone.

"I stopped by the dentist's office," the chief said. "The docs still hadn't shown up to work. The receptionist is concerned. She said she was about to call the police station to report her unease." With facial muscles sagging, the chief took off his hat, ran his hand over his hair, and placed the hat back on his head. "I'll go have a look. Wait here."

The chief disappeared around the back of the house and after five minutes passed, Angie started down the driveway. "I don't like this. I'm going to see where he is."

Courtney and Jenna trotted after their sister.

As they came to the end of the drive, the chief came around the side of the manor house and stopped when he saw the girls. His face was pale and his jaw tight. He seemed to be shaking slightly.

"What is it?" Angie asked edging towards the man.

"I called for the investigatory team."

Barely able to breathe, the girls waited for him to say more.

His voice gravelly, Chief Martin said, "Dr. Chase and Dr. Streeter are dead."

Courtney let out a gasp.

The man removed his hat and used the back of his hand to wipe the sweat from his brow.

Angie stepped to the chief and put her arm around him. "Did you go inside?"

"I looked through the window, from the back porch." Chief Martin's breathing was fast and shallow. "Listen, I don't want you to go in there. It isn't a good thing to see. The team of investigators will be here soon. Can you...?"

"Do you want us to look through the windows?" Courtney asked.

"No." The chief was adamant. "I'd like you to get close to the house, maybe stand near the front and see if you can sense anything. Just stay near the front. Don't go around back."

"Okay. Should we know anything else?" Angie asked.

"I'll tell you more later. Don't go in back," the chief repeated.

Angie started for the house with Courtney and Jenna hurrying after her. No one said a word. When they crossed the front lawn, they stood at the steps of the place looking it over.

Flowerpots and window boxes were filled with impatiens, greens, and geraniums. Small rose bushes lined the perimeter of the large house. Hydrangeas bloomed along the fence. The home had been freshly painted.

Angie glanced over at the blue sports car. She let her eyes roam over the garage and then she returned her focus to the house. The front door didn't seem to have been tampered with. "I'm going to sit on the steps for a minute."

Courtney gave a nod. "I'm going to walk back and forth along the front of the house." She muttered, "This is as close as I'm going to get."

Jenna walked over to the sports car and then moved around the front yard. In the past, she'd been able to pick up feelings from a crime scene and was attempting to do that now.

The girls tried to settle themselves and even though their hearts were racing, they tried to push their nervousness aside to clear their heads to be open to sensations that might linger on the air.

Angie wished Mr. Finch was with them. The older man could sometimes see flashes of what had happened during a crime. Because the investigators would arrive any minute and they would have to clear the area, Angie closed her eyes to block out any distractions. Worried they would run out of time, she couldn't feel anything except her own distress. She slowed her breathing concentrating on taking in air through her nose and letting it out through her mouth. Images began to float in her mind.

Angie sensed the morning sun climbing over the horizon. Dr. Carlie Streeter, petite and slim with dark chin-length hair and bright blue eyes, finished her coffee and packed her sandwich and yogurt into the lunch bag. Her husband, Marty Chase, came into the kitchen and spoke to Carlie as he picked up his briefcase, set it on the center island, and riffled through it. He pulled out a folder, looked it over, and shoved it back into the leather satchel.

The doorbell rang.

Marty went to answer it.

The image blurred and flashes of red and orange flooded Angie's vision. She startled when someone called her name.

"Angie." Jenna was on the stone walkway standing in front of her. "The police team is here. We need to go."

Giving her head a shake, Angie stood, feeling weak and unsteady. Jenna took her arm and they walked along the driveway.

"Someone rang the doorbell," Jenna told her twin sister.

"I heard it in my mind. Dr. Chase went to answer it, but then my vision faded." Angie rubbed at her temple. A headache usually came on after she'd sensed things about a crime scene.

"That's all I got, too." Jenna noticed Courtney

staring at the blue car by the garages and she and Angie walked over to it. "What's up?"

"This car." Courtney let her eyes roam over the shiny vehicle. "You feel anything from it?"

"I don't, no." Jenna looked to Angie who shook her head.

"I do," Courtney almost whispered. "But I can't tease out what it is."

Chief Martin waved them away from the car. "Time to clear out. The team is about to get started."

Walking to their cars, the chief said, "Can I come by the house later this afternoon so we can debrief?"

A time was set to meet at the bake shop and as they headed to their vehicles, Courtney couldn't help taking one more look back at the blue car parked near the garages of the two murdered dentists.

3

It was late afternoon when the four Roseland sisters, Mr. Finch, and Chief Martin gathered around a small table in Angie's Sweet Dreams Bake Shop. The bakery-café had closed for the day and raspberry scones were baking in one of the ovens sending the delicious aroma floating over the air, but unfortunately, the group hadn't arranged the meeting to enjoy good food and conversation. With coffee and tea and a plate of cookies in the center of the table, the chief cleared his throat and started to speak.

"Every investigation is tough, but this one is particularly rough. The dentists had only moved their practice to Sweet Cove a little over six months ago. They bought the house at the edge of town around the same time. I'd met them a few times. They seemed like nice people, eager to involve themselves in the community." The chief lifted his mug of steaming black coffee and took a look out the window of the shop. "Summer's almost here. The town is bustling. Things should be happy and optimistic."

Ellie fiddled with the ends of her long, blond hair. Discovering the family had paranormal powers had been hard on her and she had a more difficult time than the others dealing with crime and murders.

The chief let out a heavy sigh and got down to business. "So ... the doctors didn't arrive at work this morning. Courtney was the first patient of the day. She and Angie became alarmed when the receptionist reported that she hadn't been able to contact Dr. Chase or Dr. Streeter. Angie called Jenna and the three of you went to the dentists' house where you ended up calling me."

"You arrived shortly after the call?" Finch asked, slowly twirling his cane in his hands.

"I did. I went to the house to look around." The chief's facial muscles tensed recalling the morning discovery.

"We waited at the end of the driveway near the road," Angie said.

"Did anything seem amiss from your vantage point?" Finch questioned.

"Nothing." Jenna held her teacup to her lips. "Nothing at all seemed out of the ordinary ... except the sensation that something was wrong."

"There was a blue sports car parked near the garages." Courtney's expression had darkened. "There's something about that car," she said under her breath.

Finch looked at the youngest sister with concern, but he didn't ask anything.

The chief glanced at Courtney to see if she would say any more and when she didn't, he went on with his report. "I walked around the front and looked in windows to see the living room, foyer, a dining room ... everything was in order. I started to think the couple had left for work and maybe, had car trouble on the way. No such luck. I went around back. There's a deck off the house." The chief paused. "I looked in one of the windows, to the kitchen. The couple was on the floor. It was clear they were dead."

No one wanted to hear any details, but they knew it was necessary in order for them to help investigate the crime. They braced themselves.

The chief said, "Their hands were bound. Their throats had been cut. They both bled out."

Ellie gasped and placed her hand on her chest.

"Were there signs of a struggle in the house?" Angie asked, her face ashen.

"There was a broken water glass on the floor. It looked like Dr. Streeter might have made an attempt to run. She was in the mudroom off the kitchen. Dr. Chase was on the kitchen floor."

"Did it seem like a robbery?" Finch asked stroking his chin.

"It appeared that some jewelry might have been removed from the upstairs dressing room. So, yes, it might have been a robbery."

Angie heard some hesitation in the chief's voice. "But, maybe not?"

"The investigators haven't shared the preliminary findings with all of us yet. I can't be sure, of course, but it looked a lot like a revenge killing to me. I won't say anymore until we hear the first reports from the team."

"Do we know any more about the doctors?" Jenna asked. "Where they came from? Why they moved to town? Any family?"

"Dr. Streeter has a sister. Marilyn Streeter. A few years older. She's on her way here from Boston."

"How old were the doctors?" Angie wondered aloud.

"From their driver's licenses, we've determined that Carlie Streeter was thirty-six and Marty Chase was ten years older." The chief drained the coffee from his mug.

"Wait." Courtney sat up to attention and asked in a worried voice, "Did they have any children?"

The chief replied, "Their receptionist told me the couple didn't have any kids."

Courtney exhaled with relief thankful that there weren't any children who were victims.

Chief Martin looked at Ellie. "The sister will arrive this evening. Any chance you can put her up here at the B and B?"

Ellie gave a quick nod. "I'll shuffle people around. Now that Tom has moved out of the carriage house, I have that apartment to accommodate guests." Tom had sold his own house and moved into one of the carriage house apartments for the few weeks before his and Jenna's wedding. Now, the newlyweds were renovating and living in a huge, old house two doors down from the Victorian.

"I appreciate it," Chief Martin said. "I told the sister to come here first to see if a room had been set aside for her."

"I'll go see to it right now." Ellie got up and hurried from the bake shop into the Victorian. When she opened the door leading to the main house's kitchen, Euclid and Circe scooted in and padded over to the shop's window, jumped up on the wide sill, and settled down to listen to the humans discuss the morning situation.

Courtney rolled her eyes at Ellie's reluctance to hear any more information about the murders. "Any excuse for her to run away from what we're talking about."

"Miss Ellie is a very sensitive person," Mr. Finch remarked kindly. "The world's horrors have a most powerful impact on her."

They're having an impact on me, too." The chief shook his head while checking his phone. "The team wants to meet with me. I'll keep you posted." He collected his things and headed for the door. "I'd like you all to come back to the dentists' house at some point." Before stepping out on the porch, he looked back at the group around the table. "I hope you know how much I appreciate all of you."

When the door clicked shut, Courtney leaned forward and crossed her arms on the tabletop. "This is a nasty one. Revenge killings? Chief Martin thinks the murders were the result of revenge?" She groaned. "Revenge about what? What could two dentists have done to make someone so full of rage?"

"It might not be revenge," Jenna said. "It might have been a random robbery. Well, maybe not random. The person must have planned it ahead of time and picked that house. The manor house is set back from the road with lots of trees around. The place is well-tended, there's a sports car in the driveway. It gives the impression that the people living there have money. It would make a reasonable target for a robber."

"The person must have watched the house." Angie swallowed hard. "The person must have been familiar with the schedule the doctors kept."

"This gives me the creeps." Courtney's blue eyes flashed. "Is someone watching our house? The Victorian gives the impression that we're wealthy even though we aren't. Someone could be planning to rob us."

"No, someone *isn't* planning to rob us." Angie's voice held a trace of tension.

"How do you know?" Courtney asked.

"Because. We'd sense it ... or something." Angie was clearly shook-up by the idea that what happened to the dentists could happen to them.

"I have the feeling the murders of Dr. Chase and

Dr. Streeter were not random and did not involve robbery," Finch said.

Everyone turned to the man with interest.

"Why don't you think it was random?" Jenna asked. "Or motivated by robbery?"

"The chief didn't come out and say it directly, but the implication was that the deaths were violent, hence he leans towards a revenge killing."

"Yeah." Courtney nodded. "I sensed anger at the house. Lots of it." She traced her finger over the table. "There's something about that car, too, but I don't know what it is." She looked at her sisters. "Did you pick up on anything about the car?"

Neither one had.

"I didn't really pay attention to it," Angie told them.

"My thoughts were on what happened inside the house," Jenna told the group.

"We need more information," Mr. Finch said. "We're grasping at straws at the moment. When the chief meets with the investigatory team, he will have more to tell us."

Angie added, "And when the sister of Dr. Streeter shows up later today, we'll learn more about the couple by interacting with her."

A knock on the bake shop door caused everyone

to jump. Courtney's boyfriend, Rufus, had his face pressed up close against the glass in the door. Betty Hayes, Mr. Finch's girlfriend, stood slightly behind Rufus and gave them a wave.

When Angie unlocked the door, the two swept in.

"We met in the driveway," Rufus explained. "We saw you through the windows."

Betty, a successful Sweet Cove Realtor, hurried over to Finch and squeezed him tight in her arms. "Victor, have you heard the terrible news about the two town dentists? It's simply terrible. Murdered in their own house."

Angie took in a deep breath. News certainly traveled fast.

Rufus pulled up a chair next to Courtney and put his arm around her. "Did you hear about it? Did you know the people?"

Courtney explained that she'd been waiting in their reception room that morning due to her broken tooth and that the doctors never showed up to work.

"Oh, my." Betty placed her hand at the side of her face. "You're a patient in their practice? Which one of the doctors is your dentist?"

"Dr. Streeter," Courtney replied.

Betty let out a little gasp. Courtney narrowed her eyes wondering if Betty would have gasped if she'd reported that her dentist was Dr. Chase.

Finch carried a chair to the table so Betty could sit. She began to babble. "Those poor people. Who would do a thing like that? Right here in our town. What is the world coming to?" Betty patted her chest. "Dr. Streeter came to see me not long ago. She wanted to put their house on the market, but needed to convince her husband to go along with selling it. She was such a sweet person." Betty took a sip from Finch's teacup and, ever the business woman, her thoughts returned to the dentists' house. "That house. It will go on the market eventually, but the circumstances surrounding the place will make it a very hard sell. A double murder in there? Oh, my, people won't like that at all. Well, I suppose the possibility exists to tear it down and build something new, if it becomes impossible to sell the property."

Finch patted the woman's hand. "No need to think about that now."

"Don't they own that blue Lamborghini?" Rufus asked. Rufus was a car lover and knew a lot about different makes and models, the auto industry, and antique vehicles. "I saw it in town the other day. Pretty flashy."

A shiver ran over Courtney's skin when her boyfriend mentioned the blue car. "I didn't realize it was a Lamborghini."

"Those two must have been raking in the money. I've seen them in a red Mercedes and a white Ferrari, too."

"Really?" Angie asked, a twitch of something pinging her senses. "They own all of those cars?"

"I should have been a dentist instead of a lawyer," Rufus lamented. "If I'd known how much you could make as a tooth doctor, I'd have switched my studies in a second."

Rufus's words swirled in the air and something about them picked at Angie like sandpaper rubbing against her skin.

4

Euclid and Circe sat side by side on the bottom step of the wide, carved staircase staring at the front door.

"The cats are making me nervous," Ellie whispered.

The Roselands and Mr. Finch sat around the dining room table eating a custard flan with fresh strawberries. Chief Martin informed them that Marilyn Streeter would be arriving after dinner and they were all interested to make her acquaintance.

"They are eager to meet this woman since she has a connection to the late Dr. Streeter," Finch said. "There's nothing to worry about, Miss Ellie. It is a sense of curiosity, not of foreboding." He hoped.

"Still." Ellie glanced over her shoulder at the

felines. "They don't usually do that, sitting there, keeping watch."

The doorbell rang and Courtney jumped up to answer. The family friends, Mel Able and Orla O'Brien, stood on the porch and when the door opened, they entered the foyer and smiled at the family.

"Hello, Roselands." Mel's booming voice echoed off the walls. Spotting the cats, he greeted them. "And hello to the two fine felines." In his early seventies and carrying quite a few extra pounds, Mel bent to scratch the cats' cheeks and loud purring filled the air as he asked them, "Have you been sitting here waiting for us? How did you know we were coming?"

"Actually," Courtney told Mel and Orla, "they're waiting for someone else."

The friends took seats at the table and Angie cut slices of the flan and passed them to Mel and Orla.

"I missed your wonderful desserts." Orla, in her late sixties with auburn curls and hazel eyes, sighed with delight at the taste of the smooth, creamy custard. "The best I've ever tasted."

Mel and Orla had met at the Victorian's bed and breakfast several months ago and the two had fallen in love with one another. Orla had paranormal powers and when she was staying at the B and B, she'd helped Ellie subdue a criminal who had broken into the house with murder on his mind. Mel and Orla also fell in love with the pretty seaside town and promised to return in the spring for Jenna and Tom's wedding and to make Sweet Cove their permanent home.

"How's the house hunting going?" Jenna asked.

"Betty has taken us around to five different places, but nothing's been right yet," Orla said with a chuckle. "I guess we're too picky."

"We have certain requirements," Mel boomed. "They haven't been met yet."

"What sort of requirements?" Ellie eyed them.

"Nothing strange, if that's what you're thinking." Mel sipped from the glass of sherry Angie had brought him. "We want to be within walking distance to the center of town ... and the price has to be within our budget, of course."

"Other than that," Orla said, "we just want a small, cozy place, nothing fancy, with a bit of a garden out back to have a picnic table, some chairs, and a little space for flowers and vegetables."

Mel sat up straight, looking proud. "The house hasn't worked out yet, but I have some news ... I am now gainfully employed."

"You got a job?" Courtney stared at the man. "I thought you were retired?"

"I am retired, however, I feel the need to be useful." He winked. "Also, a part-time job keeps me out of Orla's hair a few hours a day." Mel's bald head shone under the light of the chandelier. "I have landed a job at the stained glass shop in town."

"Francine's place?" Jenna asked.

"That very store." Mel nodded.

"Do you have experience in stained glass?" Finch asked.

"None at all, but I have painted, made jewelry, and I know my way around a pottery wheel. Francine thinks I'll be able to pick up the art of stained glass in no time at all. In the meantime, my duties include waiting on customers, preparing objects for shipping, taking orders, and the like. I started this morning."

"Francine is lucky to have you," Jenna told Mel with a smile.

"Congratulations on your new job." Finch raised a glass and the others happily joined in. "What about you, Miss Orla? Do you have plans to find employment?"

Orla dabbed her lips with her napkin. "Not right away. I've been so busy for years, I'd like to find a home, do some decorating, get us settled. Then maybe I'd like something part time."

"Is there something in particular you'd be interested in doing?" Finch asked.

"I was a hair stylist many years ago. I also did skin care." Orla pushed a curl from her eyes. "I dropped into Gloria's salon the other day and we had a chat. She said she knew all of you very well." Gloria owned and operated a hair salon in town and despite having some paranormal powers of her own, she didn't talk about them and was very discreet about her "skills."

"So," Mel said, taking a look over to the staircase. "Who are the cats waiting for?"

"A new guest," Ellie said. "She should be arriving any minute."

"Friend or foe?" Mel raised an eyebrow.

"That's to be determined," Angie told them.

"You heard about the murders in town?" Jenna cut Mel another piece of the flan and set it on his plate.

Orla's eyes darkened. "We did. Everyone in town is talking about it. Are you giving the police a hand in the matter?"

"We are." Courtney nodded.

"Let me know if there's anything I can help you with." Orla made eye contact with the Roselands.

"The woman we're expecting is the sister of the murdered dentist, Carlie Streeter." Angie picked up her glass. "She'll be staying here with us for a few days."

"Well." Mel placed his fork on his plate. "I'm glad you told us. I'll be careful about what I say to her."

"Perhaps we should head to the carriage house," Orla suggested. "The poor woman would probably be more comfortable without a lot of people sitting around the table."

As soon as the words were spoken, the cats meowed and Euclid arched his back. A second later, the doorbell sounded.

Everyone exchanged looks and Ellie rose slowly and moved to open the door. Mel and Orla said goodnight and headed out the back way to their carriage house apartment.

A tall, slim woman in her mid-forties came into the room pulling a rolling suitcase. She held a caramel-colored leather briefcase in her other hand. Her hair was blond and cut short in layers around her face and she had on a blue skirt and a yellow short-sleeved shirt with a blue suit jacket hanging over her arm. The woman's manner was direct and to the point. "I'm Marilyn Streeter. People call me Mari. Police Chief Martin said a reservation had been made for me here."

"Yes, come in." Ellie introduced herself and led the woman to the table. The family greeted Marilyn and offered her some refreshments which she refused. Ellie brought the registration forms and asked the new guest to fill them in. "We're very sorry about the loss of your sister and brother-in-law."

The muscle in Mari's jaw tightened. "Thank you." She wrote quickly over the forms while Ellie explained about breakfast, afternoon snacks, and all-day beverages. "In the summer, we have drinks and appetizers out in the garden three evenings a week."

"I'll need to work while I'm here," Mari said. "Is there a spot in the house besides my room where I can have some space to work?"

"What do you do for work?" Mr. Finch asked pleasantly.

Mari turned her blue eyes on the man and answered without expression. "I'm a physicist. I teach at a university in Boston and also do work at a lab in California."

"How very interesting. Perhaps we could chat sometime while you're here." Finch smiled.

"Perhaps." Mari turned to Ellie. "So is there somewhere I can work?"

Ellie led the woman to the sunroom. "We have a quiet sunroom off the living room and there's a library on the second floor. I'll show you."

When they were out of earshot, Courtney kept her voice low when she said, "She's not very friendly."

The cats growled low in their throats.

"She is here under difficult circumstances," Finch said. "She probably needs her privacy right now."

Angie had been quiet while the woman filled in the forms. A wave of unease had washed over her when Mari arrived at the Victorian, but she couldn't sort out what it meant.

"A physicist," Finch remarked with admiration. "The Streeter siblings were well-educated, ambitious people."

"Mari is about ten years older than her sister," Jenna observed. "I wonder if they were close."

"Hopefully, we'll get a chance to talk with her." Courtney stood up to clear the table. "If she's willing to give us some of her time, maybe we'll learn a few things." Stopping before heading to the kitchen, she said, "Was Mari in Boston this morning?"

Everyone turned to Courtney.

"I wondered the same thing." Angie gathered some cups to take to the dishwasher. "Our new guest doesn't seem that broken up about the loss of her sister."

"Chief Martin will find out where Mari was this morning." Jenna helped her sisters with the dishes. "I'll head home after we clean up. Tom won't be happy to hear we were at the scene of a double murder today."

With the two cats following behind him, Mr. Finch leaned on his cane and carried the flan dish in his free hand to the kitchen. "There are many questions that need to be answered before the puzzle can begin to take shape. I hope to have a chance to speak with Dr. Mari tomorrow." Finch's eyes twinkled. "I thought of having breakfast here in the morning."

"Good idea, Mr. Finch." Ellie came into the room. "Come early, in case Mari is an early riser. She's settled in her room now. I tried to engage her in conversation, but she wasn't interested. She was eager to get to work in the library." Looking from sister to sister, she said, "If one of you had passed away, I would be so distraught I wouldn't be able to think straight. I'd be in tears for months. This woman seems hard and uncaring."

"People handle grief in different ways, Miss Ellie," Finch said. "Perhaps the two women had a falling out and weren't close or the age difference may have been such that they never formed a strong bond. Relationships can be very complex and complicated."

Ellie sat at the kitchen table with her elbow on the tabletop, her chin in her hand, and a faraway look on her face. "What did you say bothered you about that car in the dentists' driveway?" She directed the question to Courtney.

"I got a strange feeling about it." Courtney paused while washing the flan dish in the sink. "It was vague, but something about that car seemed off. It made me feel creepy."

"When is Chief Martin coming over?" Ellie asked.

"He isn't coming over tonight." As soon as she spoke, Jenna's eyes widened and she turned around and stared at Ellie as Angie's phone buzzed with an incoming call.

From on top of the refrigerator, Euclid let out a low hiss.

Angie picked up her phone, saw who was calling, and while carrying it out to the back hall to answer, she gave Jenna a look that said, *she did it again.*

Although Ellie denied it, she had the uncanny ability to sometimes anticipate a phone call or a visit from someone.

When Angie returned from speaking on the phone, her face was covered with a tense expression of worry. "It was Chief Martin. He has something to talk to us about. He's on his way over."

Jenna raised an eyebrow and frowned. "I guess I won't be going home just yet."

ngie got the fire pit going so the heat of the blaze would chase away the slight chill in the night air. The sisters and Mr. Finch decided to talk outside with Chief Martin to keep the conversation private in case Mari Streeter wandered downstairs.

The stars glimmered in the inky sky and a half-moon glowed creamy white. Angie thought what a pleasant night it would be to sit near the fire with drinks, roast marshmallows, and make s'mores ... if their gathering was a social one, which it wasn't.

Mugs of coffee and tea were passed around and everyone pulled up Adirondack chairs. Circe sat on Mr. Finch's lap and Euclid stretched out next to Courtney, the two of them squished together in the seat.

The chief cleared his throat and looking over to Courtney, he said, "You were right about the car."

Anxiety pulsed through Angie's veins and she tensed waiting to hear the news.

"The investigators went over the house and the garages and they popped the trunks on the vehicles." He paused. "There was a body in the trunk of the blue car."

Ellie gasped louder than the others did.

"Do you know who it was?" Jenna gave a shiver.

"Not yet. It's a young man, maybe in his late twenties, short brown hair, dressed in jeans, sneakers, and a buttoned-down shirt. None of us recognized him from the area. He didn't have a wallet, no ID on him."

"What was the cause of death?" Angie asked with a concerned tone.

"Undetermined as yet. No visible gun shot or knife wound. We're waiting on the medical examiner for more information."

"Have you told Mari Streeter about this?" Courtney questioned. "Maybe she could identify the young man."

"I haven't spoken with her yet." The chief's expression told them it was not a task he was looking forward to. "I have a meeting scheduled with her early in the morning at the station. The news hasn't been provided to the press so she shouldn't hear anything until we meet, but maybe it would be best if I come here instead of having Dr. Streeter come to the station tomorrow. I don't want her to overhear anyone discussing the new information, should it leak out."

"We can tell her in the morning that you'll be coming here to talk with her." Angie nodded.

"This discovery adds another dimension to the case," Finch observed. His hand moved gently over the black cat's soft fur.

"It certainly does." Chief Martin let out a long breath.

"I wonder how long the young man was dead?" Jenna thought out loud. "Was he in the car's trunk *before* the couple was killed ... or *after*?"

"Did that car belong to the couple?" Ellie asked.

"Rufus said he noticed the car in town the other day," Courtney informed the chief. "Could they have just purchased it?"

"The ownership of the car is being looked into as we speak."

"If it was a new purchase, was the body in the car when they brought it home?" Courtney asked. "Or, did the *dentists* kill that young man?"

"I didn't think of that," Angie said slowly, a look of disgust on her face.

Euclid raised his head and growled deep in his throat.

"When the young man is identified, it will help determine some common threads between people." Finch adjusted his glasses. "At least, I hope it will."

"I do have some information on the couple." The chief removed his small notepad from his back pocket and flipped it open. "Dr. Carlie Streeter was born and grew up in Connecticut. Her parents were both teachers. Both have passed away. She had the one sister, Mari. A smart girl, Carlie excelled in her high school classes and was a track star. She went to UPenn on a running scholarship, graduated summa cum laude with a 4.0 average, then went to dental school at Harvard."

"How did she meet her husband?" Jenna asked.

"They met when Carlie was doing her clinical practice work. Dr. Chase was about ten years older. They started dating when Carlie graduated and the two decided to open a practice together in New Hampshire. They stayed there for almost nine years. Just about six months ago, they moved their practice to Sweet Cove and bought the manor house."

"Do you know why they moved here?" Finch asked.

"Not yet." The chief set his mug down on the grass next to his chair. "I hope the sister can shed some light on these kinds of questions."

"I had an appointment with Dr. Streeter about six months ago," Courtney told the group. "She asked me a lot of questions about myself. I couldn't talk very well with my mouth wide open so she could check my teeth, but I asked her where she'd lived before. She told me the same things, that she'd grown up in Connecticut and had moved here from New Hampshire. When I asked what prompted the move, she only said that they wanted a change. I didn't realize it at the time, but now when I think back, she was evasive in her answers to the few questions I managed to ask."

"That's interesting," the chief said. "Did you just have the one appointment with her?"

Courtney nodded. "Just the one visit."

Chief Martin told the group, "We'll be interviewing the receptionist at the office and the dental hygienists. We'll talk to people in New Hampshire, try to find some of the couple's friends. You know the drill. Talk to whoever you think would be helpful. If two of you would sit in on my meeting with Dr. Streeter tomorrow, I'd appreciate it."

"What about the husband? Dr. Chase?" Finch adjusted in his seat so the sleeping black cat wouldn't slip off of his lap. "Have you found any information on him?"

"A little bit. He grew up in central Massachusetts, went to dental school at Tufts. He was a nationally-ranked archer in high school and college. In his last year of college, he was in a car accident and broke both arms. Dr. Chase never regained his skill in archery. He set up a practice in Boston, met Carlie, and they moved to New Hampshire."

"Does he have any relatives?" Angie asked.

Chief Martin gave a nod of his head. "Only his mother, she's in her late sixties. She's been informed and will be arriving in town tomorrow. She is still living in central Massachusetts. The father is dead. No siblings. We'll be talking to the mother and with former patients, associates, friends, anyone who knew the man." The chief rubbed his chin and the side of his jaw. "I'd like to share some details of what appeared to have happened in the manor house."

Ellie stood up so fast her chair almost tipped over. "I think I should go inside. I've heard enough for now. I don't want to listen to any more of this."

"It's okay," Angie spoke gently to her sister. "Go on in. If there's anything we think you need to know, we'll give you the important parts and leave out the details."

Relief washed over Ellie's face as she bolted into the house. "Thanks."

"Some things never change," the chief said with a sympathetic smile. "So.... as far as we can tell, the morning started as usual for Drs. Streeter and Chase. From the conditions of the house, it seems the two got up, showered, dressed for work, ate breakfast. Dr. Streeter's briefcase and lunchbox were in the kitchen. Dr. Chase's briefcase was in the hall by the front door."

The chief sucked in a deep breath. "As I mentioned, when I went around the back of the house, I looked in the windows. Dr. Streeter was on her back in the mudroom just off the kitchen near the rear door. Her hands were bound. Her throat was cut."

Jenna, Courtney, Angie, and Mr. Finch made sounds of disgust and shock.

The chief went on. "I broke the glass in the door and went inside. I checked for Dr. Streeter's pulse. She was dead. I went into the kitchen. Dr. Chase was also on his back and was dead from the same circumstances that had befallen his wife." The chief paused to collect himself. "I've seen my share of terrible things. It never gets easier. It appeared that Dr. Chase had been dragged into the kitchen. Probably, Dr. Streeter attempted to run and was caught and killed by the assailant. There was no sign of forced entry."

"So, the doorbell must have rung and Dr. Chase went to open the door." Angie leaned forward in her seat as she tried to piece together the information.

"Maybe he knew the person and let him in," Jenna speculated. "If he didn't know the person who rang the bell, he must have opened the door anyway. It was morning. He might have thought the person had car trouble and needed help or was there for some other legitimate reason."

"The attack must have been quick." Courtney looked off across the dark yard. "The killer must have known who lived in the house and what their morning routine was like."

"Any indication if the killer arrived at the manor house on foot or by vehicle?" Finch asked.

The chief shook his head. "We don't have an answer for that. Yet."

"Was a weapon found at the scene?" Jenna's mind was twirling from idea to idea.

"No, and it seems the attacker might have worn gloves, but differentiating the fingerprints found in the house will take some time."

"It was planned then." Angie sorted through what was known. "There's no sign of forced entry, the person brought a weapon, he must have known who lived in the house and when they left for work, and he was careful not to leave fingerprints." She looked to Chief Martin. "Was blood found anywhere else in the house?"

"Only in the hallway from the foyer to the kitchen."

"Isn't that odd?" Angie narrowed her eyes. "Killing someone like that ... there would have been a lot of blood. If it was a robbery and he went upstairs to steal jewelry, wouldn't he have tracked some blood through the house?"

"Even if he didn't go upstairs, if he killed them and fled ..." Courtney surmised, "he would have left traces or drops of blood where he walked."

The chief asked, "How can that be explained?" The family knew the chief was quizzing them to get them thinking.

"He cleaned up his footprints before leaving the kitchen?" Finch asked.

Jenna's eyes went wide. "He might have been

wearing some protective clothing, probably booties, too. After he killed them, he removed the plastic raincoat or whatever he had on and left the house being careful where he walked."

"But," Courtney said, "if the killer was wearing a plastic coat, wouldn't Dr. Chase think that was odd and not let him in?"

"Or...." A woman's voice spoke from the shadows near the house. "The attacker killed the two people and then he, and he alone, traveled back in time five minutes prior to when he stood on the front porch about to knock on Carlie and Marty's door." Mari Streeter stepped over to the fire pit. "And by going back in time, instead of *knocking* on the door, he turned and made his escape."

Everyone stared at the physicist ... with their mouths dropped open.

6

"The killer traveled back in time?" Jenna cocked her head and her voice sounded doubtful as if Mari Streeter might be mocking them.

Mari sat down next to the chief in the chair Ellie had vacated. "You don't believe it's possible?"

"No, I don't." Jenna gave the woman a suspicious look.

"People believe that time only runs in one direction." Mari glanced at the people sitting around the fire pit. "Forward, into the future. But, physicists have studied this extensively using computer simulations and mathematical calculations, and new theories arise. In one theory, put simply, particles in the universe were tightly condensed before the Big Bang. After the Big Bang, the system expanded outwards, but in *two* different directions ... with time moving forward and, in an alternate universe, time moving backwards. Time can run both forwards and backwards and events in the future can influence the past."

No one knew what to say, so Mari went on. "Another theory tells us that our universe cycles through four different phases which would also allow time to move in both directions."

"These theories suggest that people can move backwards in time?" Angie asked.

"Possibly." Mari folded her hands in her lap. "What an interesting ability that would offer up. Think of the possibilities." The woman let out a long breath. "I could go back in time, take my sister and brother-in-law out of the house on the morning of the murders, and when the killer shows up, the house is empty."

"If only," Mr. Finch said wistfully.

"But time travel would open up a number of problematic issues." Angie's head was practically spinning from thinking of time moving in two directions. "The killer could go forward in time and find your sister. Multiple actions by multiple people would change the future, things would constantly be changing, it would be chaos." Shaking her head, she said, "I don't buy it ... despite physicists' theories and experiments. Theories are one thing, reality is another. Time moves in only one direction. It is what it is."

Mari said, "It takes time to wrap your head around new information. Open your mind. You may be surprised at what you discover."

Courtney said quietly, "You'd be surprised at what we've opened our minds to over the past year since moving to Sweet Cove."

Angie gave her sister a withering look warning her not to say a word about their paranormal skills.

Mr. Finch headed off any questions from Dr. Streeter as to what Courtney might have meant. "The topic is fascinating. I'd like to learn more about it if you could suggest some books that a lay person might understand."

"I certainly can." Mari looked pleased by Finch's interest. "I'll write down some suggestions for you."

Chief Martin cleared his throat and addressed his question to the physicist. "Could I speak to you inside the house for a little while? I have some information to share."

Mari let out a sigh and stood. "No time like the present, I suppose." Her voice held a tinge of sadness.

The chief looked to Angie. "Can we use the sunroom?"

When Angie nodded, the chief led the way into the Victorian and after they'd disappeared into the house, Jenna said, "That was mighty weird. Does Mari Streeter believe that stuff she was saying to us? I don't mean the scientific aspect of it. Does she think people can actually travel back in time?"

"Was she playing with us?" Courtney sounded indignant. "Was she trying to prove how smart she is? Was she trying to freak us out? If she was, then why would she do that? Why is she talking about particles and theories instead of being sad about her sister? She sure doesn't seem too broken up over Carlie getting murdered."

The cats sat up and listened closely to the conversation.

"As I said earlier, perhaps the women weren't close," Finch observed. "Perhaps Dr. Streeter sees the world logically, in only scientific terms. She might be ruled by reason. She may have no room in her life for emotion."

"That would be terribly sad." Courtney frowned. "What do you think, Angie?"

Angie blinked. The conversation had made her feel slightly ill. "I don't know what to think. That whole interaction made me uneasy. I *am* willing to open my mind to unexpected possibilities. We've been doing that ever since we moved to Sweet Cove. But, I'm not going to just accept what some woman I've never met says to me about scientific theory. I'm careful and skeptical, I need some proof. I need to know more before I'd even consider anything like time travel."

"That's very reasonable, Miss Angie." Finch rubbed his hand over the top of his cane.

"And why does she not show some emotion over her sister?" Angie went on. "It's a life lost, a life that was taken, snuffed out too soon. Even if she wasn't close to her sister, isn't the loss of a life something to feel sorrow over?"

"I think she's weird," Courtney confided softly. "Her sister died this morning and she comes out here and talks to us about time travel. Sheesh."

Finch said, "If you told people that someone like Miss Ellie had the ability to move objects in space without touching them, would they have the same reaction you had to Dr. Mari's comments?"

Jenna sighed. "Yes, but they'd be skeptical unless they saw it with their own eyes. At least our skills happen in *this* universe, not in some parallel thing."

"And anyway," Courtney said, "the killer

certainly isn't some scientist who has mastered the ability to move through time. So the whole discussion is irrelevant to the crime."

A shiver of anxiety ran over Angie's skin. *It better be irrelevant.* Accepting her family's paranormal skills had been hard enough. She couldn't wrap her mind around time travel and she wasn't going to try. If Mari Streeter wanted to accept that possibility, she was free to do so. "Let's concentrate on helping to solve this crime through normal means."

Courtney raised an eyebrow and chuckled. "You mean through *our* normal means."

The two cats lifted their chins and trilled.

"What do you think about the young man in the trunk of the car?" Jenna put her feet up on the stonework surrounding the fire pit. "No obvious cause of death."

"And what's his relationship to the dentists?" Angie asked.

Courtney said, "Hopefully, the police will be able to identify him, and then we can talk to people who knew him."

Chief Martin came into the backyard. "I've given Dr. Streeter the new information about the young man in the car. She has no idea who it could be. I kept it short. Our morning meeting is still on. I hope some of you can sit in with me."

"Did Mari say any more about time travel?" Courtney frowned.

"Thankfully, no. I have no idea how to respond to any of that. If she wants to believe time travel played a role in the deaths, she is free to do so, but I intend to go about the investigation leaving out an inquiry into traveling back in time." Chief Martin gave a little smile. "I don't have the manpower for that."

The people around the fire pit let out chuckles.

"We agree with you," Angie told the man. "We're going to leave that possibility to Mari and focus our attention on other things."

"I need to get home before Lucille divorces me for never being around." The chief lifted his jacket from the chair he'd been sitting in earlier. "I'll see you in the morning."

The family wished him goodnight and the conversation turned to other topics.

"I need to get busy filling jewelry orders." Jenna was a jewelry designer and she sold her wares out of a shop at the back of the Victorian, at stores in town, and on the internet. "With the wedding and then our short vacation, I'm way behind. I need to buckle down and get back on track."

"I can help you after the bake shop closes for the day," Angie smiled. "I can start tomorrow."

"I can help tomorrow evening," Courtney told her sister.

"I can't make jewelry, but I'd be glad to help package the items for shipment," Mr. Finch nodded.

"That would be great," Jenna said. "I knew I could count on all of you ... and there's nothing like free, experienced help."

"Who said anything about working for free?" Courtney kidded.

"We don't come cheap, you know," Angie warned.

"You get what you pay for, Miss Jenna," Finch chimed in.

"Well, you can send me your bills and I'll see what I can do." Jenna finished off the tea in her mug.

"It is time for me to go home." Finch gently moved Circe from his lap and pushed himself up out of the chair. "Miss Betty is coming over for coffee and dessert."

"A late night visit?" Courtney winked at the older man. "Well, well."

They couldn't see it in the darkness, but Finch's cheeks turned pink. "Miss Betty often works late hours so we get together when she is free." He lifted his cane.

"I'll walk you home, Mr. Finch." Courtney took the man's arm and the two strolled along the stone pathway that led from the Victorian's backyard into Finch's property. Finch had installed the walking path and some lights when he purchased the house behind the Roselands. The cats jumped down from the seats and followed along.

"I'll help carry in the mugs and then I'll head home, too." Jenna gathered some of the cups.

"It's odd not having you in the house with us," Angie told her twin with a touch of sadness in her voice.

"I'm only two houses away," Jenna said, "but it *is* strange not to be living under the same roof with all of you. We'll adjust though."

"Change is never easy." Angie picked up the other cups and they headed for the back door.

Jenna turned around to pick up her sweater from the back of her chair and when she straightened, something caught her eye under the pergola on the side of the yard by the flower beds. So surprised by what she saw, she lost her grip on one of the mugs and it hit the patio with a crash.

Angie spun around to see the broken cup on the

ground. When she shifted her focus to Jenna, her eyes widened and she followed her sister's gaze. "What's wrong?"

It took several seconds for Jenna to answer. "Over there, under the pergola."

"I don't see anything." Angie's voice was soft.

Jenna's shoulders shook. "It's gone now."

"What was it?" Angie squinted in the darkness.

Jenna looked at her sister with a serious expression. "A young man. He was staring at me."

Angie stepped closer to Jenna.

"He looked all shimmery." Jenna touched her hand to her face. "He disappeared, like the light inside of him was fading." She slipped her arm through Angie's and pulled her close. "Angie, he was a ghost."

7

After seeing the ghost, Angie and Jenna went inside and found Ellie in the kitchen. She took one look at them and alarm flashed over her face as she stepped across the room to their sides. "What happened? What's wrong?"

Jenna sat down at the island and put her head in her hands. "I saw a ghost."

Ellie stiffened, but she kept her voice calm. "Where?"

"In the garden under the pergola." Jenna's breathing was quick.

"Did you recognize him?" Ellie put her hand gently on Jenna's shoulder.

"No. I've never seen him before."

"Did he speak?" Ellie asked.

Shaken, Angie sat at the center island on the bar stool next to her twin. She admired the calm and rational way Ellie was asking for information ... like seeing a ghost in your yard was a normal thing.

"No. He just looked at me." Jenna pushed her hair back from her face.

With the two cats leading the way, Courtney came through the back door from walking Mr. Finch home and when she saw her three sisters, she knew something was wrong. "What's cookin'?" she eyed them with suspicion. When she heard about the ghost under the pergola, she went to the kitchen window to look out into the darkness. "A ghost? In the yard? Cool. I wish I saw him."

Euclid and Circe jumped up to the top of the refrigerator and meowed.

Rubbing at the tension in her forehead, Jenna took a deep breath.

Ellie went on with the interrogation. "Did you sense anything from him?"

Jenna blinked, thinking back on the happening. "He ... seemed like he wanted something. Maybe."

"What did he look like?" Ellie asked.

Jenna said, "Mid to late twenties. Short hair, brown. A slim build. He had on jeans and a light blue button down shirt."

Angie's eyes went wide and she opened her mouth to speak when Courtney, excitement bubbling in her voice, said, "It's the guy from the car at the dentists' house. The dead guy in the trunk. It must be him. It's the same description that Chief Martin gave us."

An involuntary shudder ran through Jenna's body. "What does he want? Why did he come here?"

"He knows you can see ghosts." Courtney took a pint of ice cream from the freezer and spooned some into a dish. "He needs something so he showed up here trying to find you."

"I don't know what to do." Jenna practically whispered. "What do I do?"

"Don't worry about it." Courtney licked her spoon. "He'll show up again."

Jenna's face paled. "I don't want him to show up again."

"We each have our skills," Courtney pointed out. "Ellie doesn't like hers either, but there doesn't seem to be anything you can do about it."

"Think of it as helping someone in need," Angie suggested trying to soothe her sister's nerves.

"One second we're heading into the house, and the next, there's a ghost in the yard," Jenna groaned. "Wait until Tom hears about this."

"He'll think it's cool." Courtney sat down at the kitchen table with her bowl of ice cream. "How come I can only sense things, but you get to see ghosts?"

Jenna looked like she'd trade "skills" with her sister in a split second.

"Don't be so worried," Courtney said. "You've seen Nana's spirit and you have a ghost living in your house."

"I've never seen Katrina though," Jenna pointed out. "I just know when she's around."

Courtney made a face. "That's creepier than *seeing* a ghost. At least when you see a ghost, you don't have one sneaking around you."

"Katrina doesn't sneak around," Jenna corrected. "She.... Oh, I don't know. I'm exhausted. I'm going home." She looked to Angie. "Can you and Courtney sit in with the chief tomorrow morning when he talks to Mari Streeter? I need a break. I want to sleep in."

"Of course. It's fine." Angie hugged her. "You've been straight out with the wedding and now, this. We'll handle the interview. Go home and rest." She was going to walk Jenna home when Ellie picked up her phone and said, "I'll walk with you so you aren't alone."

When Jenna and Ellie left the kitchen for the

front door, Courtney asked without looking up, "Did Ellie take a 'make-me-brave' pill or something?"

Angie chuckled. "I was wondering the same thing."

Courtney raised her blue eyes to Angie. "What's with this ghost? Why did he show up here?"

Letting out a long sigh, Angie said, "I have no idea."

"I was trying to make Jenna feel better about seeing the ghost, but this is..." Courtney shrugged a shoulder. "Concerning."

Like a cool breeze, a flutter of nervousness blew over Angie's skin and goosebumps raised along her arms. The family had been so happy the past month preparing for Jenna and Tom's wedding and the day of their vows was so beautiful, fun, and full of joy ... and ever since Josh had proposed to her, Angie felt like she'd been floating on a cloud.

She marveled at how everything could shift in a matter of seconds.

∾

COURTNEY AND ANGIE joined Chief Martin and Mari Streeter in the sunroom and when the door was closed, everyone was seated, and the reason for the two sisters sitting in on the interview was explained, the chief started the conversation.

"I'd like to ask some questions about your sister and her husband."

Mari looked stern and stiff. She ignored the chief's comment and instead, looked from Courtney to Angie. "You have experience in police investigations?"

"Yes," Angie replied thinking giving too much information would result in more detailed questions.

"How so?" Mari tilted her head in question.

"We consult on certain crime cases." Courtney sat up straight keeping her facial expression serious and using a tone of authority.

"Why? What can you do to help? What sort of experience do you have?" Mari demanded.

"We do a great deal to help," Courtney told the woman. "We have well-honed skills that can cut through hidden agendas, evasive answers, and concealed motives. We've helped solve crimes here in Sweet Cove and in other areas of the state."

"What is your training?" Mari narrowed her eyes.

Courtney leveled her gaze at the woman. "Our training and experience are really only relevant to the police department and they have asked us to consult. Law enforcement's confidence in our skills should be testament to what we can do."

Mari was about to ask something else when Courtney cut her off. "Why don't we focus our attention on the crime and how best to solve it." Courtney looked over to the chief and gestured for him to go on.

Angie loved how her sister handled situations like these and she admired how articulate and professional Courtney could be.

The chief addressed his question to Mari Streeter. "Can you tell us about your sister's upbringing?"

Mari exhaled loudly and told the chief and the sisters want they already knew about Carlie, that she was intelligent, hardworking, sweet, got along with everyone, was a track star, went to the University of Pennsylvania and then on to dental school.

"Had Carlie always wanted to be a dentist?" the chief asked.

Mari scoffed. "I have no idea what Carlie wanted. My parents encouraged her to pursue a career that would provide prestige, money, and respect. My parents struggled financially even though they had good jobs. Our father spent money like a drunken sailor. He wanted fine things, things that cost more than he could afford. He impressed the importance of financial security on us from the time we were little kids. That's what mattered to him. Money ... and lots of it."

"Did Carlie seem unhappy with the demands?" Chief Martin asked.

"Carlie was like clay, you could mold her into what you wanted her to be and she didn't say boo. The girl had no backbone. Maybe she didn't know what she wanted because our father always decided for her."

"What about your mother?"

Mari rolled her eyes. "That's where Carlie came from. The two of them were cut from the same cloth. Our mother didn't have any opinions, she dedicated her life to being pleasant and smoothing things over. She didn't like conflict of any kind."

"What about you?" the chief asked. "Did your parents influence your choice of career?"

Mari smiled. "Good luck with that. I got the same lectures from our father ... be a doctor, be a doctor. Well, I guess I fulfilled his demands because I *am* a doctor, although a Ph.D., not a medical doctor like he wanted me to be."

"Would you describe your relationship with your sister as close?"

"I would not." Mari's jaw was firmly set.

"Were you in contact with one another?" the chief asked.

"Rarely." Mari glanced out of the windows to the backyard's green lawn and flower gardens. Her jaw muscle twitched. "I went to their wedding, Carlie sent me Christmas cards."

"Had you seen Carlie since her wedding?"

"No."

Chief Martin asked, "How long ago did she marry Dr. Chase?"

Mari waved her hand around. "Oh, I don't know … about six years ago, maybe?"

Angie had to suppress her shock that the two sisters hadn't seen each other in over six years.

"Had you spent much time with Dr. Chase?" the chief asked. "Did you feel you knew him well?"

Mari leaned against her chair back. "I really didn't know him at all."

"The couple had no children?" Courtney questioned.

"That's correct," Mari said. "No kids."

"Did your sister want children?" Angie asked.

Mari tilted her head. "What does that matter now?"

"We're trying to gather information to create as

clear a picture of your sister as possible, her interactions, her hopes, what was important to her, what wasn't, her habits," Angie explained. "These kinds of things can point the investigation in different directions."

Mari didn't reply.

"Did your sister report or hint at anything being wrong?" Courtney questioned. "Was the couple happy together? Was there any trouble with a neighbor, someone at work, a friend or acquaintance?"

"Like I said, we rarely talked. Sometimes Carlie would give me a call, we'd chat for a few minutes, but honestly, I never knew what to say to her." Mari took a look at her watch. "I need to get some work done. I don't think I can be of any help to you."

Chief Martin gave a nod. "If you don't mind staying in Sweet Cove a few more days, I'd appreciate it."

Mari was about to stand up when the chief reached down to his briefcase and withdrew a manila envelope. "I'd like to show you a photograph. The young man in it is the person who was found in the trunk of the vehicle on your sister's property. There are no marks of violence on the body. Would you be able to take a look at the photo in the hopes you might recognize him?"

Mari swallowed. "I can look at it." She squared her shoulders and extended her arm.

Chief Martin removed an eight by ten photograph from the envelope and handed it to the woman.

Angie saw something pass over Mari's face as one of her eyebrows raised slightly and she swallowed hard. Mari handed the picture back to the chief. "Never saw him before."

Chief Martin thanked Dr. Streeter and informed her that they might need to talk again. Mari stood, nodded at the three people, and walked deliberately out of the room.

Angie asked to see the photograph and Courtney looked at the image over her sister's shoulder.

The brown-haired, slender young man appeared as if he was asleep except for the pale, pearly white skin and the dark circles under his eyes.

Angie's stomach clenched. *So this is what Jenna's ghost looks like.*

8

Angie's employee, Louisa, stood next to a café table talking to a young man about thirty-years old who was enjoying a mocha latte and a slice of lemon cake. Louisa, fit with slight curves, had long, jet black hair with the tips dyed a bright blue. She was an efficient, smart, hardworking woman who had been in a lousy relationship and vowed never to allow that to happen to her again.

When she sidled up to Angie with shining eyes, she asked, "Do you know that guy? He's cute, isn't he?"

Angie glanced over to the table. "He sure is and he hasn't taken his eyes off you since you waited on him, but no, I don't know him."

"No matter how cute he is, I'm being careful."

Louisa put a hand on her hip. "There won't be any more bad relationships for me. I'll never be a pushover again." Taking a carton of milk from the refrigerator, she added, "That murdered dentist seemed like a pushover and look what happened to her."

Angie turned to Louisa. "Dr. Streeter? Was she your dentist?"

"Yeah, I thought she was sweet." Louisa shook her head and her face clouded. "Who would kill her? Do you think it was a robbery or did someone target her and her husband?"

"I have no idea. I didn't know either dentist. What was Dr. Streeter like? Why was she a pushover?"

Louisa said, "Dr. Streeter was really nice, always cheerful, but she seemed like she did whatever her husband told her to do. He seemed like the boss in the office. Maybe it was the age difference between them."

"Did she seem unhappy around him?" Angie asked.

"One time I was in the dentist chair waiting for her," Louisa said. "I could hear her husband chewing someone out in the back office. The door was closed so I couldn't make out what he was saying, but his tone was angry and sort of mean-sounding. After a few minutes, he opened the door with a bang and stormed out. A minute later, Dr. Streeter came out. She looked upset. She came in to check my teeth and she wasn't her usual self. I resented Dr. Chase after that. I never liked him. He seemed arrogant, bossy, full of himself." Louisa scowled as she went to wait on a customer.

A tall, good-looking man entered the bake shop and when Angie glanced in his direction, she smiled from ear to ear. Josh Williams, her fiancé, took a seat at the counter and beamed at his sweetheart.

"I just got back from New York." Josh sipped the coffee Angie placed in front of him. "I couldn't wait to get out of those meetings. I was counting the seconds until I could come home and see you."

Angie asked how the business dealings went and Josh gave her the highlights of his two days in the city.

"Have you heard the news from here?" Angie asked.

Josh's face lost its smile. "What news?"

Angie told him about the murdered dentists, the sister of the dead woman, and the unusual conversation about time travel. Josh stared at Angie for a few seconds wondering if she was making the story up to tease him, but then he knew it was the truth.

"How can this be? A double murder? A body in a car?" Josh's mouth pulled down at the corners. "Time travel?"

"There's another thing." Angie looked around to be sure no one was listening and leaning closer, she lowered her voice. "Jenna saw a ghost in our backyard. He looks like the young man who was found in the trunk of the car. We think its him."

Josh was one of the few people who knew about the Roselands and Mr. Finch's special skills. "I've only been gone two days," he said in amazement. "All this happened in just two days?"

"Two very long days." Angie touched Josh's hand and smiled at him. "I'm glad you're back."

"So am I." Josh held Angie's eyes. "That diamond ring sure looks pretty on your finger."

Angie lifted her hand so the light sparkled off the diamond engagement ring. "It does, doesn't it? It was a gift from a very nice man."

"Anyone I know?" Josh kidded.

"You might know him. He comes in here sometimes."

A man sat down on the stool next to Josh. "Will

you two stop mooning at each other? It's embarrassing."

Angie turned to see Jack Ford, a Sweet Cove attorney and Ellie's boyfriend, perched on the stool dressed in a summer-weight, pale gray linen jacket and a yellow bowtie. "Jack, I didn't see you come in."

"That's because you were making goo-goo eyes at this man next to me."

Josh swiveled and smiled at Jack. "And you don't make goo-goo eyes at a tall, pretty blond that I know?"

"Never in public." Jack sniffed. "Public displays of affection are inappropriate for a professional person."

Angie narrowed her eyes and gestured. "Is that why, not long ago, you and Ellie were caught kissing right outside the bake shop window?"

Jack blushed.

"In fact," Angie went on, "I distinctly recall some of the customers knocking on the window and others applauding your kiss."

"Say no more," Jack groaned. "You've made your point."

Angie brought over a cup of coffee and a piece of banana bread with chocolate chips and placed them in front of Jack.

Josh said, "I asked Jack to come along with us to Robin's Point. I want to run another idea past you about the land and I thought Jack would be helpful since he knows the town rules and regulations."

"Okay, sounds good. I'll be ready in about forty-five minutes." Angie left the two men to chat while she finished up with the customers and completed the end of day tasks with Louisa.

When the bake shop had been locked up, Angie, Josh, and Jack rode in Jack's sedan the short distance through town to Robin's Point. The point was a bluff of land that jutted out into the ocean that had once been owned by the Roselands' relatives. Josh owned the Sweet Cove Resort and Hotel which had been built on part of the point and when he and his brother bought the land to develop, they left open acreage that included a small park with a path leading down through the dunes to a sandy beach for the townsfolk and tourists to use.

When they'd parked and walked to the center of the bluff, Josh unrolled the paper with the preliminary plans for moving the park's location slightly and dividing the remaining land on the point between the four Roseland sisters.

"I had the thought to change the layout a bit." Josh turned the diagram. "If we adjust the lots like this, then everyone has more of an east-southeast orientation which will give better views and sunshine for more hours of the day."

"That's a great idea." Angie walked the area trying to imagine four cottages on the spot. "We wouldn't want to build anything big. Just small cottages, probably one-story, that sit nicely on the point and fit in with the landscape."

"Those are the sorts of cottages that were here initially," Jack said, "before the town basically forced the owners off the land." Unfortunate misdeeds of the past had led to the cottage owners having to give up their little homes and the town eventually sold the parcel to the Williams brothers to develop the space.

Tears glistened in Angie's eyes. "Nana would be so happy that the land was being returned to the family."

Josh put his arm around his fiancée. "The land on the point should never have been taken from her. I wanted to make things right."

"Thank you." Squeezing his hand, Angie leaned in and kissed her husband-to-be.

Jack walked around the bluff. "I don't see any problem with orienting the lots the way you suggest. The town would have no objections to how it will be sub-divided." Turning to Angie, Jack said, "Ellie told me you were there when Chief Martin found the bodies of those dentists. I went to Dr. Chase for my dental care. He was an excellent dentist."

Angie suspected that Jack wanted to say something more.

"But there was something about the man that I didn't like. So much so, that I was planning to leave the practice and go elsewhere."

"What made you uncomfortable?" The breeze blew a strand of Angie's honey-blond hair into her eyes and she pushed it aside.

"He had an arrogant manner. The man was disrespectful of others, he treated the staff rudely. I didn't care for the over-bearing way he treated his wife." Jack adjusted his bowtie as they walked back to the car. "I thought I should mention it. I told Ellie, but she gets very emotional about death and I wanted to be sure you knew what I'd observed. I could see Dr. Chase getting into trouble if he rubbed the wrong person in the wrong way."

Angie thanked Jack. "I've recently heard something similar from someone else."

"The whole thing is horrible." Jack shook his head slowly. "There are times when I almost lose faith in humanity."

Josh put his arm around the attorney's shoulders. "We can't do that, Jack. We can't let the evil-doers win."

Jack gave a nod of his head as Josh turned to see where Angie was.

Angie stood a few feet behind the men, looking over to the resort spread out over acres of lushly landscaped grounds at the edge of the promontory.

"Angie?" Josh called to her.

Angie blinked and faced Josh and Jack, her face looking tense and worried.

"Is something wrong?" Josh asked.

Standing with her arms hanging limply by her sides and her shoulders rounded, Angie said in a quiet voice, "Yes ... but I don't know what it is."

9
___

"I felt like something was pulling at me." Angie gestured towards the resort. "It felt like the pull was coming from the resort."

Josh stared blankly across the green lawn at the buildings that made up the seaside hotel. "What would have caused the sensation?"

"I don't know, but it sure drew my attention."

Jack looked puzzled, his forehead scrunched and his blue eyes inquisitive. "Shall we go over and see what the cause might be?"

They walked to the front entrance of the Sweet Cove Resort and entered the elegant lobby where groupings of sofas and chairs clustered around the large, high-ceilinged room. A stone fireplace stood on the far wall and the lighting was soft and flattering.

"The feeling has subsided." Angie pressed her fingers against her temple. "Whatever bothered me seems to be gone."

Josh headed for the reception desk and spoke with one of his employees. "Did someone check-in within the last ten minutes or so?"

"No one." The man behind the granite counter was dressed in the resort uniform of black slacks, a pressed, light grey shirt, and a dark plum-colored necktie. "But someone came in a few minutes ago who was here before. He was here early in the morning when those dentists got murdered."

"He was here that morning? What did he want?" Josh asked.

The desk clerk leaned forward. "That morning the man said he was supposed to meet someone in one of our cottages. He said an associate was supposed to reserve one of the bungalows. There wasn't anything under the name he gave. The cottages were all filled so I described the suites and rooms that were available. The man seemed very distracted, he took a look at his watch and said he had to go. He turned around and left in a hurry. The same man was just here again a few minutes ago."

"What did he want this time?" Josh asked.

"He asked if anyone else besides him had come

looking for his associate the other morning. I told him that no one had."

"What did this man look like?" Josh questioned.

"About mid-thirties, medium build, looked fit. He had dark blond hair, he was dressed business casual."

"Had you seen him before the morning of the murders?" Angie moved closer to the desk.

"I don't recall seeing the man before," the desk clerk said.

"Did he happen to tell you his name?" Jack spoke in an official-sounding voice.

"He didn't, no."

"What was the name of his associate?" Josh asked.

"Mr. Kravetz."

"Did this man arrive by car? Did you happen to notice if he got into a vehicle when he left?" Josh glanced out of the glass door as if he thought the man might still be nearby.

The desk clerk looked crestfallen. "I'm sorry, I didn't notice how he arrived or how he left."

"Thank you," Josh said to his employee as he took Angie's elbow and moved towards a sofa and two chairs.

"I think my unease must have been because of

the man who was looking for his business associate." Angie kept her voice down.

"Who could he be?" Jack kept looking around the room in case the man returned.

"That's the million-dollar question." Josh looked at Angie. "Are you feeling better?"

"I am. My concern left with whoever that man was." Angie slipped her hand in Josh's. "Jack and I should head back to town. The chief is expecting Dr. Chase's mother to arrive early this evening and he wants me and Courtney to sit in on the interview."

"I'll walk you back to the car," Josh said. "If that man is important, you'll figure it out."

Angie was pretty sure the man looking for his associate in one of the resort cottages would provide some important information to the case of the murdered dentists ... *if* she was able to find him.

"I RAISED Marty on my own. My husband died when my son was only a year old." Mrs. Chase, Marty's mother, sat at the conference table in the police station across from Courtney and Angie. Chief Martin sat at the end of the old, fake wood table writing some notes.

Jack had dropped Angie at the Victorian just as she received a text from the chief informing her that Dr. Chase's mother had arrived from central Massachusetts.

Greta Chase was in her late-sixties and gave the impression that she was energetic and intelligent. A petite woman with a few extra pounds, her silvery-blond hair was cut in a chin-length bob and she wore gray slacks and a navy jacket. She folded her hands in her lap. Her eyelids were tinged red ... Angie assumed from bouts of crying over her dead son.

"Marty was my only child." Mrs. Chase dabbed at her nose with a crumpled tissue. "He was always a handful, full of energy, couldn't sit still, was always on the move. Marty was so smart, everything came easy to him. He was valedictorian of his high school class, went on to college, and then to dental school."

"Were you and Marty close?" the chief asked.

Mrs. Chase let out a long breath. "I had to be a disciplinarian with Marty. He was high-spirited. He had an attitude and I don't know where he got it. My son could be arrogant. I don't think he was unkind, but he focused on himself a good deal and sometimes was so engrossed with his own needs and wants that he forgot about other people's feelings.

He wasn't a bad boy, but if you gave him some rope, he'd hang himself with it. I had to keep my eye on him at all times. It was exhausting."

"I understand he was a talented archer," Angie said.

"Oh, yes. I put him in archery so that maybe he'd learn some self-control. He learned it, but he only demonstrated it when he had a bow and arrow in his hands. Self-control didn't carry over into the other areas of his life. He was always impulsive, didn't take the long view of things."

"He was in a car accident?" the chief asked.

Mrs. Chase shook her head sadly. "That accident ... it was a turning point. Marty lost his desire to excel at archery. His injuries were severe. He didn't want any part of the long, slog back to his championship form. He abandoned the sport. He struggled with addiction to pain killers. I demanded that he go into treatment. He came out clean and went to dental school." The woman wrung her hands. "You asked if Marty and I were close. Our relationship consisted of me nagging him to be his best and to stay out of trouble and him dragging his feet to reluctantly meet his challenges. I loved my boy, but our relationship was a difficult one."

"What did you think of Carlie?" Courtney asked.

Mrs. Chase smiled. "Carlie was a sweetheart. Smart, kind, loving, hardworking."

"But...?" Courtney waited for the woman to go on.

"But she wasn't a good match for Marty. Marty needed a firm hand and Carlie was too soft. Marty walked all over her. I didn't like it. Her gentle nature allowed Marty's disagreeable side to run wild." Mrs. Chase said, "I hate to say so, but my son could be rude and selfish and arrogant. The older he got, the more that side came out."

"Was Marty in trouble with anyone?" the chief asked.

Mrs. Chase looked surprised. "I have no idea."

"Do you know why the couple left New Hampshire and came to live in Sweet Cove?" Angie asked the woman.

"If I had to guess, I'd say Marty might have needed a change. He might have run his mouth off or annoyed people in some way. Maybe they lost friends because of Marty's behavior. Maybe he got himself into trouble with someone. I really don't know. A fresh start in a new place could have looked like a good idea."

"You mentioned Marty had become addicted to pain killers after his car accident." Chief Martin made eye contact with Mrs. Chase. "Did he ever show signs of being back on drugs?"

Mrs. Chase blinked a few times. "I never thought he was. I didn't see him much though. I hope that hadn't happened. I think Carlie would have told me."

"Your son had some expensive automobiles," the chief said.

"His Mercedes?"

"He had a Lamborghini and a Ferrari."

Mrs. Chase's eyebrows raised. "I didn't know about the Ferrari."

"Those are very expensive vehicles," Chief Martin noted.

"Marty always loved cars." Mrs. Chase seemed to be thinking about her son's possessions.

"The house they purchased in town was also quite expensive."

Angie eyed the chief.

Chief Martin asked, "Did your son or his wife inherit any money that you know of?"

"Inherit money? No. Carlie's parents had passed away years ago. There wasn't anyone to inherit money from."

"Was your son an investor?"

"I think he had some mutual funds." Mrs. Chase

nervously adjusted her necklace. "I didn't know him to be much of an investor. Marty preferred to spend money, not save it. Maybe Carlie took their finances in hand and made some good investments?"

"That could be." The chief nodded and then shifted in his seat. "I have to share some other news about what was found at the couple's home." He went on to tell the woman as gently as he could about the body in the trunk of the car.

Mrs. Chase gasped and placed her hand on her stomach. "Who was he? The young man in the car?"

"We haven't made an identification yet." Chief Martin hesitated and then asked if she would be able to look at a photograph of the man to see if she could identify him, explaining that there were no upsetting signs of foul play on the body.

"I guess so." Mrs. Chase's cheeks flushed pink.

When the photograph was passed to the woman, she held it gingerly, took a look, and then passed the picture back to the chief as quickly as she could. "I don't know him." She watched as the photo was slipped back into its manila envelope. "How did he die? What was the cause of his death?"

"Overdose," Chief Martin told her. "Opioids."

"Drugs," Mrs. Chase said. "You don't know who the man is?"

"Not as yet. He doesn't match any missing persons reports. He isn't known in town. It will take some time, but we're confident he'll be identified."

Mrs. Chase's facial muscles tensed. "Did that man kill Marty and Carlie?"

"The coroner puts his time of death around the same time as the attack on Dr. Chase and Dr. Streeter."

Mrs. Chase said in a shaky voice, "Then the same person probably killed him *and* my son and daughter-in-law."

"The investigation is ongoing. We don't yet have anything concrete to link the deaths."

Yet.

Anxious sparks of electricity jumped over Angie's skin as she exchanged a look of worry with her sister.

10

Angie and Josh rode side by side on their bikes along the paved trail that ran for miles along the ocean. The day was warm and dry with a brilliant sun shining against the azure blue sky dotted with a few puffy white clouds. Angie had been telling Josh about the interview with Dr. Marty Chase's mother last evening.

"In plain English, the guy sounds like a real jerk." Josh kept his eyes on the path ahead. "I'm sorry to put it so bluntly and I know his mother described him as having been hyper and inattentive and kind of wild, but the guy doesn't seem to have felt the need to ever modify his behavior."

"I was surprised the mom was so forthcoming about how difficult Marty was to raise," Angie said. "And about how difficult his personality could be."

"Marty seems the type who could get himself into trouble pretty easily." Josh took a look at Angie. "Did you believe what the mother was saying?"

"I did. It all seemed very sincere. Marty was not an easy child. It sounded like she'd done her best to try and put him on the right path forward."

"Seems he might have messed things up," Josh noted. "Did Marty get into trouble with someone? Was he back on drugs? Did the medical examiner do toxicology tests on Marty and Carlie?"

"They did. The results aren't back yet."

Josh and Angie pedaled along admiring the beautiful scenery of the coast, the crashing waves, the expanse of ocean mirroring the color of the sky, the sandy dunes, the fragrant pink and red rosa rugosa blooming along the path. Angie wished they could forget about crime and murder and misdeeds, but it was impossible to push it very far from her mind.

"Has the chief looked into the dentists' finances?" Josh asked. "It seems like they were spending their money like water. I know they must have made huge salaries from their practice and maybe they invested well, but that house? And those cars? They would have blown through their money pretty fast at the rate they were going."

Angie pondered, "I wonder if they spent so extravagantly when they lived in New Hampshire."

"That could be telling." Josh weaved around a rock on the path. "If their spending started when they moved here, what was different? Where did they *suddenly* get all the money?"

"If they spent the same way when they lived in New Hampshire," Angie said, "where were they getting the money to spend so lavishly for so long?"

Josh raised an eyebrow. "It could be that the couple was supplementing their income somehow."

"Illegal stuff?" Angie asked.

"Possibly, or maybe they had rental properties or other streams of income. The police must be thinking the same things that we're thinking. They'll look into it and figure it out."

"That could help us unravel the strings of the case." Angie shifted gears on the bike. "One thing could lead to another."

The two bicyclists pulled off the trail and parked the bicycles. Josh removed a blanket from the pack on his bike and Angie unsnapped the small cooler containing their lunches. They walked to the edge of the bluff to eat and rest and admire the view.

"What do you think of what you've heard about

Carlie Streeter?" Josh took a long swig from his water bottle.

Angie unwrapped her sandwich, thinking about her response, and she lifted her eyes to Josh. "You know, I have a feeling that Carlie wasn't as passive and malleable as she's being portrayed."

"You've heard the same report from different sources though." Josh removed a cookie from the container and gave Angie a sheepish grin. "I can't resist these cookies you made so I'm eating my dessert first."

Angie teased, "You know that's very naughty, don't you?"

Josh winked as he bit into the chocolate chunk sweet. "It won't ever happen again."

Angie chuckled. "We'll see how long that promise holds."

Josh leaned back on the blanket and watched the birds fly overhead. "What makes you think Carlie was different from how she's been described?"

Angie finished her sandwich and put the container back into the cooler. "I can't point to anything specific. It's just a feeling I have. Think about it. Carlie was super smart, she excelled at her studies, excelled at track. Could a weak-willed person do all of those things just because someone else expected them to?"

Josh gave a shrug. "I have no idea. I think if someone was so demanding about what I needed to do, I'd become resentful and maybe sabotage my activities to show I couldn't be pushed around. I know that would be really dumb, but, who knows how we'd react in a situation like that."

"I find myself feeling a connection to Carlie." Angie redid her ponytail to contain loose strands of hair that had fallen out. "I know I often appear to be very compromising and concerned about my sisters and Mr. Finch. I want things to go well for them, I try to smooth things out for them. It's probably because I'm the oldest."

Josh chuckled. "Well, you beat Jenna being born by a few minutes so yes, you are the oldest in the family."

Angie went on. "So I bet people think I'm sort of weak or impressionable or easy to manipulate."

Josh adjusted his position on the blanket, leaned on his elbow, and looked Angie in the eye. "Those things you do for your family aren't signs of weakness and anyone who thinks so is ignorant. You, Angela Roseland, are not only one of the finest people I've ever known, you are also one of the strongest."

Angie's throat tightened with emotion as Josh pulled her close and pressed his lips against hers. When he came up for air, he told her, "If anyone on earth thinks they're luckier than me, they're wrong because the best person I know has agreed to spend her life with me."

Angie touched Josh's cheek and kissed him.

After finishing lunch and resting in the sun, the two went back to their bikes and got ready to continue their ride. While attaching the lunch box to the bicycle, Angie looked over at Josh. "You know what? I don't think Carlie Streeter's father or Marty was able to push her around. I think she did what she wanted to do, what she needed to do. I bet she ran the household *and* the dental practice. Maybe she wasn't overt about it, but I bet quietly and in a low-key way, Carlie ran the show."

"You could be right." Josh's face was serious as he gave the idea some thought. "That's an interesting take on the couple."

Angie swung her leg over her bike and they took off up the path. "Everyone is looking at Marty, his expensive taste, his drug addiction, his difficult personality, his selfish nature, implying that something he did may have resulted in the couple getting killed." Making eye contact with Josh, she asked, "If the reason they got killed had to do with something one of them had done, was it something Marty did ... or was it something Carlie did?"

Josh stopped his bike and stared at Angie. "Meek little Carlie's actions get dismissed and everyone focuses on Marty. That's an excellent point. You could be on to something."

"I know that law enforcement will look into both of the dentists' lives, their contacts, friends, finances, and important details will come out that could lead the police to the killer." Angie rubbed at the tension in her neck. "But there's some sort of worry tugging at me."

Josh searched Angie's face. "Can you tell what the source of the worry is?"

"Not yet. Maybe it's just because all of the information is swirling around and I can't put it in any order." She gave Josh a little shrug and they continued on their way.

Ideas about the couple raced through Angie's brain. She needed to have conversations with people and she wanted to hear more news from Chief Martin. Who was the man in the trunk? Did Dr. Chase and Dr. Streeter know him? Who did the blue sports car belong to? If it was owned by the dentists, who did they buy it from? Angie wanted to know more about the couple's finances and where all their money was coming from. Was Marty using drugs again?

A new thought popped into her head. Was Marty selling drugs? He probably had contacts in the drug world from when he was using opioids himself. As a dentist, could Marty get his hands on drugs to sell by writing phony prescriptions? Angie needed to contact some employees who worked for the dentists and she wanted to talk to people the couple had known when they lived in New Hampshire.

The off-road bike pathway ended at a two-lane road and the path picked up again on the other side about a hundred yards up the street. Angie and Josh stopped their bikes and looked up and down the road. Seeing that it was clear of any traffic, they rode across and pedaled along the side of the street heading for the bikeway entrance. In the distance, the sound of a large truck rumbled behind them.

A pang of anxiety flared in Angie's chest causing her to pedal faster. The engine sound of the truck got closer and Angie felt like it was bearing down on them. With her heart pounding like a drum, she stood up on her pedals and pumped as hard as she could.

"Hurry, Josh!" She yelled behind her.

The thundering of the truck pummeled against Angie's eardrums as she moved her bike swiftly off the road and onto the trail with Josh right on her tail.

Breathless, the two stopped their bicycles and looked back as the truck roared past, sideswiping the brush and vegetation on the side of street where Angie and Josh had just been riding.

"That guy wasn't paying any attention. He must have been texting on his cell phone." Josh was indignant. "If we were on that road for two more seconds, he would have killed us. We made it onto the bike path just in time."

Sweat trickling down her back, Angie stared after the truck. She could hear it roaring away down the road.

Some of the words that Josh had just said pulsed in Angie's brain as a chill raced over her skin. *Time. Seconds.*

11

The Roseland sisters, Tom, and Mr. Finch sat outside at the wooden dining table under the newly extended pergola eating their dinner of creamy pasta with salmon, grilled vegetables, and green salad. The cats ate plain fish and vegetables from small plates placed on the grass. The sun was setting, the air was warm and pleasant, candles flickered on the table, and Ellie's garden was bursting with colorful flowers blooming in the beds. Lighted torches ringed the periphery of the garden glimmering in the growing darkness.

Sitting under the pergola, Jenna kept looking over her shoulder. They were sitting right where she'd seen the ghost standing and staring at her the other evening and, being in the same spot with night falling, sent a shiver of nerves over her skin.

Angie had been telling the family about the truck that almost mowed her and Josh down as they rode bikes a short distance along the country road to pick up the bicycle path. "It was frightening. I felt the hot whoosh of air as he roared past us. We'd just made it to the trail. It shook us up and kind of put a damper on the rest of our ride."

"The driver must have been on his phone or was adjusting the radio," Finch surmised. "He probably didn't even see you."

A shudder ran over Angie's shoulders. "I think you're right. We were lucky to make it to the trail before he blew past us. The truck ran up along the side of the road into the brush before he realized he was leaving the street and corrected his position."

"Too bad you didn't get the license plate number," Jenna said.

"The buffoon should lose his driver's license." Tom's face was red with anger. "He shouldn't be allowed to drive."

The cats looked up from their dinner and hissed as the ruff of fur around Euclid's neck puffed up making him look even bigger than he was. Circe's tail flicked back and forth.

"Thankfully, nothing happened." Angie blew out a breath. "We returned safe and sound. I just want to forget it." She looked over at Tom and smiled. "The vegetable kebobs are delicious. Compliments to the grillmaster."

The chat turned to everyone's businesses and how things were going now that the tourist season was kicking in. Tom told them about a new construction project he was excited to be working on. "It will give my company some nice word of mouth advertising."

Mr. Finch and Courtney reported on a new fudge flavor they'd attempted and they wanted the group to sample some for dessert to give their opinions on the taste.

"What are you calling the new flavor?" Ellie asked reaching for the bowl of salad.

Courtney said, "It doesn't have an official name yet, but it's a combination of marshmallow, graham cracker, chocolate, and caramel. It's sort of our take on the camp- side summer s'mores."

"My mouth is watering," Tom announced. "Can't wait to try them."

"I made something for dessert, too," Angie told the family. "It's a lemon chiffon freezer cake."

"I'm going to gain five pounds tonight." Tom chuckled, as he patted his tummy. His happy face lost its smile and the others followed his gaze to see what had caused the swift change of emotion.

Chief Martin walked into the backyard from the driveway. "Evening. Sorry to bother. I rang, but no one answered so I thought I'd check back here."

"It's no bother." Angie stood up. "Have you eaten? We have plenty of food. Join us."

The chief started to make excuses about why he shouldn't interrupt the gathering when Jenna said, "You should know by now that you're always welcome here with us."

"I bet you haven't eaten for hours." Ellie pulled over another chair.

"And I bet you could use a drink." Tom removed a beer from the cooler and handed it the chief.

Courtney went inside and returned with another place setting.

"Lucille is out with her sister. I haven't eaten since breakfast." Chief Martin eyed the pasta and vegetables. "It sure smells good."

"Sit," Angie said. "No excuses. You can't run yourself into the ground."

"You must take care of yourself, Phillip." Mr. Finch passed the bowl of creamy pasta to the man. "You have to keep up your strength, especially during such difficult and disturbing cases as this one."

Angie's heart started to race when she realized the chief must have come to tell them some news. Wanting him to have a break from his work and knowing he'd speak about it eventually, she didn't ask him anything about the murdered dentists.

After he'd eaten his dinner, sampled the desserts with everyone, and finished his beer, Chief Martin took a deep breath and placed his napkin on the table. "Thank you for a terrific meal and for the enjoyable company."

Letting out a sigh, he said, "I assume you know why I came by." He looked from face to face. "I have some information to share. The team has identified the young man in the trunk. His name is Jeremy Hodges, age twenty-nine. Estranged from his parents. His girlfriend, Tara Downey, went to the police because Jeremy hadn't come home the night before he died and he didn't show up at work on the day of the murders. Jeremy and Ms. Downey shared an apartment together in Miltonville, New Hampshire."

"Does he have a connection to the dentists?" Courtney asked.

"He does indeed." The chief gave a slight nod.

"The young man was a dental hygienist. He worked for Dr. Chase and Dr. Streeter when they had their practice in Miltonville."

"Ms. Downey told you this?" Jenna asked.

"She did. She came down to talk to us." The chief took a sip from his water glass. "The couple had been together for about two years. Ms. Downy is a nurse practitioner. She and Jeremy met in university while studying for their respective careers. Mr. Hodges worked at another dental office for about five years and then moved to the Chase-Streeter dental office."

"Did his girlfriend mention any trouble between Jeremy and the dentists?" Ellie asked.

"She reported no trouble at all. Jeremy liked his job with Dr. Chase and Dr. Streeter."

"Why was Jeremy Hodges in Sweet Cove?" Angie questioned.

"No one knows the answer to that. No one alive anyway."

"Had Jeremy kept in touch with the dentists?" Mr. Finch leaned forward.

Chief Martin said, "Ms. Downey said she didn't think he had. She reported being shocked to learn that Jeremy and the doctors had been killed. She appeared distraught when she was talking to me, but it seemed forced."

"You say that as if you're suspicious of her," Tom observed, his eyebrow raised.

The chief gave a shrug. "I'm suspicious of everyone. Present company excluded, of course."

"Did Jeremy have a drug problem?" Ellie shifted uncomfortably in her chair.

"The girlfriend says no. Jeremy was against drugs. She said he had nothing to do with drugs at all. She was adamant about it. Ms. Downey does not believe he died from an overdose of opioids. She said it was impossible."

"If he wasn't doing drugs," Angie said, "then did someone kill Jeremy by injecting him with drugs causing an overdose?"

"A possibility," the chief nodded.

"What about the blue car?" Courtney asked.

"The car had been purchased by Dr. Chase and Dr. Streeter from a car dealer in Sudbury three days prior to the murder. The dealer has all the paperwork. Everything is in order."

"Did the dealer know Jeremy?" Finch asked.

"I brought some photographs of the young man to show the dealer. The salesman said he'd never seen Jeremy before."

"He could be lying," Tom said.

"He could be," the chief acknowledged. "But I didn't get the sense he was lying to me."

"Did the salesman say anything about the dentists?" Angie's mind worked on the new information. "Were they acting like everything was okay? Did they get along with each other during the purchase of the car?"

"The guy said they seemed like a normal married couple. He said Carlie didn't want to buy the car. He heard them arguing about it out in the lot. The salesman reported that Marty came back alone a few days later and bought the car." The chief frowned. "Not a whole lot to go on there."

"How did Jeremy Hodges get to Sweet Cove?" Ellie's brow furrowed in thought.

"We're not sure. Jeremy's car was parked in the lot of the New Hampshire dental office where he was working presently. He didn't show up for work that morning, of course, but the staff noticed his car was in the lot. The office staff called Tara, the girlfriend, to ask where Jeremy was and if he was okay. That sealed Tara's worry and she went to the police."

Everyone sat quietly pondering the news.

"What about the dentists' finances?" Jenna asked. "Where were they getting all their money?"

"The dentists had a very healthy income from

their dental practice and they'd made good invest-ments." The chief paused.

"There's something more?" Tom guessed.

"A certified public accountant is looking into it for us. We always have suspicions when someone is blowing a lot of money, but they need to be confirmed. The couple could have been spending every dime they brought in. They may have been overextended with loans." Chief Martin looked around the dark yard and at the blazing torches with their flames dancing in the occasional evening breeze. "If their lavish spending was supported by loans and mortgages, it would be impossible to sustain such an expensive lifestyle for much longer."

"Were they involved in something illegal?" Finch pushed his eyeglasses back up his nose.

"Unknown." The chief's face looked tired and drawn. "Hopefully, we'll learn something soon."

"Do you think Jeremy went to see the dentists about something and ended up being in the wrong place at the wrong time?" Courtney asked the ques-tion that had gone through everyone else's heads. "Do you think he walked into the murders and ended up getting killed because he was a witness?"

"It's possible," the chief said. "A strange coinci-dence though, isn't it? The young man comes down from New Hampshire and shows up within seconds of the couple's attacker? I don't know." He shook his head. "I just don't know."

As a shiver of unease washed over her, Angie's throat tightened at the chief's words.

"There's more to it than that, don't you think?" Jenna asked, her voice tinged with tension.

The chief's jaw tightened. "If I had to guess? Yes, there's more to it than coincidence. I don't think that Jeremy Hodges just happened to walk into the Chase-Streeter home at the exact time the two doctors were being murdered."

Angie's sinking heart told her the chief was right.

12

Tara Downey was in her late twenties, petite, and athletic-looking. Her short, brown hair had blond highlights running through it and her big brown eyes shone with intelligence. At Chief Martin's request, Tara had come to the B and B to talk with Angie and Jenna. The three sat under the pergola at the wooden table with large glasses of iced tea in front of them and a platter of cookies and sliced fruit in the middle of the table. Euclid and Circe sat in the shade listening to the conversation and watching the newcomer carefully.

After giving the young woman their condolences, Jenna and Angie began their questioning.

"Was Jeremy friendly with Dr. Chase and Dr. Streeter?" Angie asked the first question.

"Jeremy loved working for them. He was upset when they decided to move to Massachusetts. He and Dr. Chase loved cars and talked about them all the time." Tara's hand shook slightly when she reached for her glass.

Jenna asked, "Did Jeremy keep in touch with them after the move?"

"I didn't think so." Tara took a long swallow of tea. It was an unusually hot day with little breeze. A bead of sweat showed at the young woman's hairline.

"You went to the police in your town after Jeremy didn't come home that night?" Angie questioned.

"I went the next morning. Jeremy didn't come home. He was usually home before me. I was surprised he wasn't in the apartment when I got back from work. I texted him over and over, but he didn't answer. Even though we hadn't had a fight or anything, I checked the closet to see if his clothes were still in there. I don't know why I did that. I had the silly idea that he'd left me and hadn't said anything to me. I texted his friend, Joe, but Joe hadn't heard from him either. I drove around town to see if he'd been in an accident or if his car broke down. I even drove by the dental office where he works. I went home and tossed and turned all night. The next morning, his office called and asked where Jeremy was. They told me his car was in the lot."

"But the night before you drove by the place and didn't see his car?" Jenna tilted her head in question.

"His car wasn't there the night before. It wasn't in the lot." Tara's face was serious. "I'm sure of that. The lot was empty."

Angie had a puzzled look on her face. "Is it possible you missed it? Was it dark when you were there? Maybe the car was in shadow?"

Tara shook her head. "It was dark, but I drove into the lot. The parking area is small. I would have seen his car if it was there. It wasn't."

"Is it possible that either Dr. Chase or Dr. Streeter called Jeremy?" Jenna asked. "Maybe asked him to come down to see them about something?"

Tara stared off across the yard, thinking about the suggestion. "I suppose it's possible. I don't know why they'd do that. I think Jeremy would have told me if one of the doctors had called him."

"Is there anyone who might have given Jeremy a ride to Sweet Cove?" Angie kept her eyes on Tara's expression.

Tara's brow furrowed. "I can't imagine who would do that. His friend, Joe, works. I had to work. If he was planning a day off, he would have told the dental office he wouldn't be in. Jeremy isn't like that. He doesn't just take off. He's responsible, reliable. He'd tell someone if he had plans to come down here, he wouldn't just up and leave."

"What were his younger years like?" Jenna asked. "I understand he was estranged from his parents?"

Tara's face hardened. "Jeremy's home life was terrible. His father was always beating him up. His parents are both drunks. They take drugs, at least they did. He hasn't been in touch with them for years. I never met them. I don't know how Jeremy turned out normal with a family like that. The things he told me." Tara's lips were held in a tight, thin line as she shook her head.

"Did he have any siblings?" Angie asked.

"He had a brother, Matt. He was about ten years older. Jeremy said his brother took off when Jeremy was about eight years old and he never saw or heard from him again. He had no idea where Matt ended up."

"A sad life," Jenna acknowledged. "But Jeremy must be very resilient since he went on to school and studied for a career."

Tara gave a nod and almost smiled. "He was. He was strong and he knew he wanted a better life than he'd had as a kid."

"You're a nurse?" Angie asked.

"I'm a nurse practitioner."

"Do you have family in New Hampshire?"

"I don't. I was an only child. My mother passed away shortly after I graduated from college. I was happy she saw me finish. I went on for a master's degree. I met Jeremy while I was studying for the master's."

"So Jeremy was working for his hygienist license when you were working on your master's degree?" Angie was trying to piece together a timeline.

"Right," Tara said. "We met at the end of our programs. Jeremy had a bunch of jobs after high school. He worked as a painter, carpenter's assistance, truck driver. He decided to go for dental hygiene because it wouldn't take as long as a four-year degree. He didn't have a lot of money and he was averse to taking loans. He wanted a professional career and the dental license was a good fit for him."

"How old was he when he started the program?" Jenna asked.

"He was twenty, almost twenty-one."

"Are you older than he was?"

"I'm two years older than Jeremy."

"He worked at a different office before moving to

Dr. Chase and Dr. Streeter's practice?" Angie questioned.

Tara reached for a cookie. "He worked for about five years at a different office. Dr. Chase and Dr. Streeter's office was closer to home and larger and Jeremy was looking for a place where he could advance. He was always talking about going back to school to get his bachelor's degree and then going to dental school. I don't know if it would have happened or not. Jeremy was always worried about money. I told him I'd support us while he went back to his studies, but he was reluctant to do that. Stability and security were important to him and he was afraid not to have a job. If he had tons of savings, he would have gone back to school in a second."

"Did you have plans to marry?" Jenna asked.

The question seemed to take Tara by surprise. "We didn't, no."

"Do you think that down the line you would have married?"

"I ... I don't know. I guess time would have answered that." Tara lifted her glass to her lips.

Angie jumped in. "Did Jeremy have a girlfriend prior to your relationship?"

Tara looked dumbfounded. "Why does that matter?"

"Just to put his life in context." Angie was deliberately evasive.

"I don't know." Tara almost pouted.

Angie and Jenna both thought it was hard to believe that Tara didn't know Jeremy's dating history.

"He never mentioned anything about dating other women?" Angie persisted.

Tara shifted on her seat. "We didn't think it was productive to talk about our previous dating experiences."

"You mentioned a friend of Jeremy's, someone named Joe." Jenna asked quickly because she got the impression that Tara might end their interview.

"Yes," Tara said. "They both love cars. They got together once in a while."

"Where does Joe work?"

Tara lifted an eyebrow. "He works at an auto body shop."

"Do you know the name of the place?" Angie smiled encouragingly.

"Top Shop." Tara gave Angie a slightly annoyed look and, anticipating the next question, she said, "It's in New Hampshire. In Miltonville, where we live."

"What's Joe's last name?" Angie kept her voice even.

"Winkler."

"How long had Joe and Jeremy known each other?" Jenna asked.

"I'm not sure," Tara said dismissively.

"Were they friends when you started dating?"

"Yes, they were."

"Are the men close in age?"

"I'd say so." Tara gave a curt nod. "They're both in their late twenties."

Angie couldn't put her finger on what was bothering her about the conversation with Tara. Something seemed off, but the sensation was vague and she wasn't able to figure out what was picking at her.

"Are you staying in Sweet Cove for a few days?" Jenna asked.

Tara sat straighter with a pleased look on her face. "Chief Martin asked if I would stay for two or three days. They'll be able to release Jeremy's body to me then. I'm staying at the Sweet Cove Resort. The police department was nice enough to pick up the tab." She picked a tiny piece of lint from her skirt.

The cats stared at the young woman.

"Do you have any questions about Jeremy's death that we haven't discussed?" Angie asked.

Again, a little flash of annoyance passed over

Tara's face and when she spoke, her voice sounded hard. "Just the same questions you have. Why was Jeremy down here? Why didn't he tell me he was coming down? Who killed him? It's very upsetting."

Giving a little nod of her head, Angie wore a sympathetic expression. "Can you think of anyone who would want Jeremy dead?"

"Of course not." Tara raised her voice when she said the words.

Angie asked gently, "Can we get in touch with you at the resort if we have more questions?"

"Why would you have more questions?" Tara demanded.

"Things come up during a case," Angie told her. "Things that need to be clarified. It's standard operating procedure, that's all."

"I suppose so. If you have to." Tara pushed her hair back over her ear. "It's difficult talking about Jeremy so please only contact me if it's very important." Standing up, she thanked Angie and Jenna for the refreshments.

"I'm sorry we had to meet under trying circumstances," Angie told her.

Mr. Finch came out of the house wearing his apron from the candy shop and walked over to greet the three women. "I just left the candy store for the day." He smiled at Tara. "Hello, I'm Mr. Finch, a friend of the family." He extended his hand to shake.

Tara kept her hand by her side. "Sorry. I hurt my wrist and thumb recently so I'm not able to shake. The doctor said I have to baby it for a while. But, nice to meet you." Tara said goodbye and headed across the lawn to the driveway hurrying to where she'd left her car.

"I hoped I'd get back in time to sit in on the interview." Finch watched the woman back out of the driveway and then he turned to Angie and Jenna with a raised eyebrow. "Too bad I couldn't shake hands with the young woman."

"Yes," Angie said. "It *is* too bad. We could have used some more information about Tara."

"She didn't seem too broken up about Jeremy." Jenna eyed her sister with a frown.

"I agree. I also get the impression she likes the attention the police are giving her." When Angie sank back down on the chair, Circe jumped up on her lap and growled low in her throat.

"You didn't care for our visitor, little one?" Angie asked the black cat.

Mr. Finch noticed Euclid sitting at attention looking down the driveway where Tara had parked her car. "I wonder how Miss Tara hurt her wrist?" He slowly turned his eyes to the sisters.

"I was wondering the very same thing," Angie told him, her eyes dark with suspicion.

They all knew this wasn't the last time they'd be talking to Tara Downey.

Angie carried a platter of breakfast breads into the dining room and set it on the sideboard. Dr. Mari Streeter sat across the table from Mr. Finch discussing different aspects of physics and each time Angie came into the room with another breakfast item or a pitcher of juice, she picked up on snippets of their conversation ... dark matter, dark energy, gravity, time and space, matter and antimatter. Angie's head spun trying to make sense of the subjects.

The table was crowded with other B and B guests who occasionally entered the discussion with a question or a comment and for the most part, they all seemed fascinated with the topics being discussed.

When everyone else had finished their breakfasts

and wandered off to their rooms or to tour the town, Mari gave Finch a nod of respect. "You are a very intelligent man, Mr. Finch. I enjoy talking with you. How did you end up in Sweet Cove running a candy shop?"

Finch was about to take a sip from his teacup, but paused and set it down. "I came to find my brother who was the original owner of the candy store."

From high on the China cabinet, Euclid stood up and let out a howl that caused Mari to look up at the animal with an expression of alarm. "What's wrong with the cat?"

"Euclid was not fond of my brother," Finch said matter-of-factly.

Angie fiddled with the plates and cups on the sideboard listening to the conversation wondering how Mari would take the information Mr. Finch was sharing with her.

"The cat knew him?" Mari asked.

"Euclid knows *of* him and does not approve of the way Thaddeus lived his life."

Mari stared at Finch trying to decide if he was pulling her leg. "Lived? Is your brother dead?"

"Thaddeus was murdered."

Mari's shoulders went back and her eyes

widened in surprise. "Was the murderer apprehended?"

"Yes."

"I'm very sorry about your brother," Mari told Finch.

"My brother was a monster. No one deserves to be killed, but honestly, I can't think of a single person who shed a tear over Thaddeus's death. I walk with a cane because of what my brother did to me many years ago. I still work at trying to forgive him, but I have not yet achieved that goal. I am an imperfect man."

Angie stepped to the table and put her hand on Finch's shoulder just as Circe entered the room and jumped onto his lap.

"Mr. Finch came to Sweet Cove to see his brother," Angie said. "And by doing that, he entered our lives and became part of our family. If there is a more perfect man than Mr. Finch, then I'd like to meet him. There isn't a kinder or more loving soul in this universe."

Circe placed her front paws on Finch's chest and leaned up trying to lick his cheek.

With a tear glistening in his eye, Finch reached up and patted Angie's hand as he stroked the fur of the sweet black cat. "Wonderful things can emerge from despair. As you can see, I am truly blessed."

Mari moved her eyes over the two people and the cat and then let out a long breath of air. For a moment, Angie thought the physicist was moved by Mr. Finch's words and the depth of emotion he'd expressed.

Mari blinked and leaned back in her chair. "Any news on the murder of my sister and her husband?"

"The girlfriend of the young man who was found in the blue car is here in Sweet Cove," Angie said. "Police Chief Martin has talked with her. Her name is Tara Downey. Does the name sound familiar to you?"

"Not at all." Mari finished off her coffee. "Does she have any idea who killed her boyfriend?"

"She doesn't, no."

"Not surprised." Mari got up and poured another cup of coffee to take upstairs to the library.

"Dr. Mari has decided to stay in town for another week," Finch told Angie.

"I'm getting a lot of work done here." Mari actually smiled. "It's actually freeing to be outside of the lab and university settings. The atmosphere here in the mansion is conducive to deep thinking and I'm making good progress on the notes for my latest book. I've practically moved into the upstairs library. Maybe I'll stay here all summer." Heading for the staircase, the woman said, "You know where to find me." Glancing at Mr. Finch, she added, "I look forward to talking with you more this evening."

When Mari had disappeared upstairs, Angie looked over at Finch. "Do you actually understand the things you're talking about with her?"

"I read some of the books she suggested. I find the topics fascinating." Finch lowered his voice. "If I hadn't worked as a psychic for so many years, I would love to have studied physics."

"Really? I don't understand it all."

"It's something like our skills, Miss Angie. Hard to fathom, but nonetheless, real and existent ... and quite marvelous." A broad smile formed over Finch's face.

Angie returned the smile. "I don't understand our skills either. Maybe someday."

Finch nodded and asked, "How is the investigation going?"

Angie sat in the seat next to the older man. "Slow. Two people who are connected to two of the victims seem emotionally absent about their loss."

"Mari and Tara Downey?" Finch asked.

"When Jenna asked Tara if she and Jeremy might

have married one day, she looked almost shocked by the question ... like she'd never considered the possibility. They'd lived together for more than two years. Marriage must have crossed her mind."

"Perhaps she wishes to remain single and never wants to marry," Finch suggested.

"I understand that, but the sense I got from Tara was that she would never consider committing to *Jeremy*." Angie rested her chin in her hand. "She almost seems indifferent to her loss." Raising her eyes to the staircase, she said, "Much like Dr. Mari in her attitude towards her murdered sister."

"Indifference doesn't necessarily equal guilt," Finch reminded Angie.

"It's not what I expect from a girlfriend or a sibling though."

"Not all relationships are like yours ... or mine. We are the lucky ones, Miss Angie."

Finches words pinged in Angie's brain. What he just said was important, she was sure of it. But how?

"Where is Miss Ellie?" Finch looked down the hallway to the kitchen. "I've barely seen her this morning."

"She overslept and has been baking and putting the guests' breakfasts together like a maniac. I stayed to help serve so she could stay in the kitchen. I'd better get to the bake shop before Louisa has my head. She and the other two employees have been handling the early morning customers so I could help Ellie."

"And I must get to the candy store or Miss Courtney will fire me." Finch winked and finished the last of the tea in his cup.

As Angie was gathering some of the plates from the table to take to the kitchen on her way to the bake shop, the doorbell rang. Mr. Finch went to answer it.

A woman's voice spoke from the porch. "Hello, is Courtney or Angela Roseland at home?"

Mr. Finch glanced to Angie and she nodded.

The woman entered the foyer and spotted Angie in the dining room. The person looked familiar to her and it took a few seconds to realize she was the receptionist from Dr. Chase and Dr. Streeter's dental office.

"I hope you don't mind that I came by." The woman bit her lower lip. "I wanted to talk to you, if you have the time."

Angie looked at Mr. Finch. "Would you stop in to the bake shop on the way to the candy store and tell Louisa I'll be there shortly?"

"Will do." Mr. Finch leaned on his cane and hurried away.

"You have a beautiful home." The receptionist flicked her eyes about the room and didn't seem to know what to do with her hands until she shoved them into the pockets of her dress. "I'm Brenda Mills. I don't think we've ever been formally introduced. I want to talk to you about Carlie and Marty. Chief Martin talked to me, but...."

"You spoke with the chief?" Angie asked.

Brenda gave a quick nod. "I'm nervous. I'm upset about what happened to them. I mean, of course I am, but...."

"What is it?" Angie walked over to the woman.

"I've been on edge the past month."

"Did something happen to make you feel worried?" Angie watched Brenda's face.

"Nothing really. Maybe I'm making something out of nothing."

"Did you share your concerns with Chief Martin?" Angie asked.

"Not really. I was afraid he'd think I was silly. I overheard someone say that you and your sisters sometimes help the police." Brenda's cheeks flushed red.

Angie's heart started to pound. "Who told you that?"

"I heard someone in the market." Brenda's eyes widened as a worried expression showed on her face. "Was the person wrong? Oh, maybe I'm...."

"It's okay. My sisters and I have some experience working with the police." Angie didn't go into detail and she hoped Brenda wouldn't ask any questions about it. "I'm happy to talk with you. Why don't we go sit in the sunroom?"

Brenda followed Angie out of the foyer and through the living room, and when they were about to enter the sunroom, she said softly, "I was so afraid something was going to happen to Carlie and Marty. And then it did."

A cold chill traveled down Angie's spine.

14

Brenda sat on the cream-colored sofa and Angie took the side chair. Huge open windows looked out over the lush lawn and gardens and let a cooling breeze into the room. A ceiling fan moved lazily overhead. Euclid and Circe strolled in and settled on the area rug.

The dental receptionist was in her early forties, had nicely-styled shoulder-length brown hair, and was short and stocky. She was dressed in a summer shift and sandals. "I've been with Carlie and Marty since they opened the practice in town. They came from New Hampshire, did you know that?"

Angie nodded.

"I loved working for them." Brenda looked out of the windows and let out a sigh. "I can't believe what's happened to them." Tears showed in the corners of her eyes, but they didn't slip over the lids and she brushed at them and blinked fast a few times. "Why would someone kill them?"

Angie held the woman's gaze hoping she'd go on without prompting. When she didn't, Angie said, "You mentioned that you were worried about the doctors?"

Brenda rubbed at her forehead as if a headache was coming on. "I was, yes."

"What caused your worry?" Angie asked gently.

"About a month ago, maybe three weeks ago, Carlie dropped and broke a mirror in the office. We laughed about it saying, uh oh, seven years of bad luck. I was helping her pick up the shards. Carlie sliced her finger on a piece of the glass and got a nasty cut. She couldn't work for a few days because of it. Then two weeks ago, they crashed their Porsche. Marty was driving, he hit a tree. Thank heavens they didn't get hurt ... it was only bruises and whiplash and that sort of thing. We had to reschedule two days of appointments because they were so banged up." Brenda lowered her voice. "Carlie told me they'd been having a heated argument in the car before they crashed. She was very angry at Marty about it."

Unease began to ping in Angie's chest. "Did Carlie say what the fight was about?"

"No and I didn't want to ask. I didn't think it was the right thing to do. Carlie and I got along great, but she was still my boss. I thought if she wanted to talk about why they were fighting then she would have told me."

"Did you notice any arguing between them in the office?"

"I did. Things started to heat up in the last few weeks. There were more fights. They tried to be discreet about it, but I noticed. They were more abrupt with one another, they were more curt to each other. I worried they would get a divorce, maybe close the office. The whole atmosphere changed. There was a lot of tension in the air."

"Carlie never mentioned why they were having a hard time?"

"She didn't say a word." Brenda's hands were curled into fists. "When I heard that Carlie had been killed, the thought ran through my head that Marty did it." She shook her head. "Then I heard Marty was dead, too. I wondered if they'd had some awful fight that caused both of their deaths. Maybe they both had knives or guns and...."

Angie asked, "What did you think of Marty? Did you get along with him?"

"I got along fine with him. He wasn't chatty. Marty had a big ego, kind of lorded it over everyone that he was a *doctor*... like he thought he was better than the rest of us." Brenda paused for a second then went on. "I always wondered why Carlie would fall for someone like that. He wasn't very nice."

"When you first started working there, did you notice Carlie and Marty arguing?"

"Occasionally. At first, I thought it was just the stress of a couple living and working together in demanding jobs." Brenda unclenched her hands and clutched them together in her lap. "But then I noticed little things between them. Marty making cutting remarks to Carlie, Carlie sometimes deliberately annoying him. They were subtle, but I saw what was going on. Like I said, the past two weeks, things seemed to escalate with more fighting going on."

"Did Carlie seem afraid?" Angie asked.

"Not afraid ... angry, like she'd had enough of Marty and didn't want to take it anymore." Brenda's face looked sad. "I should have talked to her about it. I wish I had."

"Did Carlie have any friends in the area?"

"I don't think so. I know she and Marty did some golfing together, did a charity event. They hadn't been in Sweet Cove very long. They both worked long hours. I don't think Carlie had the time to get out and meet people yet."

"Did she mention any friends from New Hampshire?"

Brenda's forehead scrunched up in thought. "I don't recall her mentioning anyone. Their work consumed their days. I know they liked to go to the theatre and museums and they did go back to New Hampshire a few times to attend charity events. They both loved cars. On weekends, they often took long drives to coastal towns, the mountains, New York."

"Did you happen to see a picture in the news of the young man who was found dead in one of the doctors' cars?" Angie questioned.

Brenda winced. "I saw it."

"Did you recognize him? Or maybe his name? Jeremy Hodges?"

"No, I didn't. I'm pretty good with names, what with being a receptionist. I don't recall ever hearing his name or seeing it written down."

"Did Carlie or Marty ever talk about a Jeremy?"

"I don't think so."

Angie tried to jog Brenda's memory. "Jeremy Hodges worked for them in New Hampshire. He was a dental hygienist."

Brenda shrugged. "I don't recall Carlie or Marty mentioning him."

"He never came down to visit with them?" Angie thought if she kept bringing Jeremy up it might ring a bell for Brenda. "He didn't drop by at the office to say hello?"

Again, Brenda shook her head.

"Do you work full time?" Angie asked the question thinking that if there was someone else who worked the front desk then that person might remember Jeremy visiting or calling the dentists.

"I work every day the office is open." Brenda modified the statement. "Well, I used to, I mean. The office is closed now. Carlie's sister and Marty's mother are going to put the business up for sale."

Angie gave a nod of understanding. "Have you lived in Sweet Cove for a long time?"

"I don't live in Sweet Cove," Brenda said. "I live in Hancock."

"What did you do before accepting the job with Dr. Chase and Dr. Streeter?"

"I was a receptionist in a medical office in Hancock."

"What made you leave that practice?" Angie asked.

Brenda blinked a couple of times. "I worked there for ten years. The doctors were difficult. The staff changed over more than a few times. I wanted to find some place with a nicer working environment."

Angie talked with the woman about how hard it was to look for a new job and the difficulty of finding a group of people who were a good fit. "I run the bake shop and my sisters run businesses. It's not always easy to deal with the public."

"My gosh, no," Brenda said. "People can be very demanding. They don't think about time pressures that the doctors have to deal with. I had to handle a good number of cranky patients who demanded to be seen instantly, complaining about their bills, making excuses about paying, and on and on." The woman rolled her eyes. "I had one man come in asking for Carlie. I told him she wasn't in. He didn't believe me. Can you imagine? Why would I lie?"

"He was a patient?"

"No." Brenda's eyes widened. "He wasn't a patient of the doctors. He wanted to talk to Carlie. I told him he should make an appointment to see her. He got angry. His face got as red as a beet. He said it was very important for him to talk to her. I kept telling him she wasn't in. He made me nervous. I thought I might have to call the police."

Little jolts of unease pricked Angie's skin. "When did this happen?"

"It was the morning Carlie and Marty got killed. In fact, it was right after you and your sister left the office."

Angie sat up. "That very morning?"

Brenda nodded. "Did your sister ever get her tooth fixed?"

Angie's mind was racing. "What did you say? Oh, yes, she did. What did this man look like?"

Brenda looked confused for a second. "Um ... let me think. He was fairly tall, had tanned skin, sandy blond hair. He was dressed nice, pressed chinos, a long-sleeved shirt. He was good-looking."

"Did he say why he wanted to talk to Carlie?"

"No." Brenda frowned. "He just wanted to talk to her. That's all he said, over and over."

"Did he want to be a patient of the practice?" Angie asked.

"I don't think so."

"Had you ever seen him before?"

"No. I would have remembered him," Brenda said.

"Did he say he was a friend of Carlie's? Did he say he knew her in New Hampshire?"

"No. He just kept saying he needed to talk to Carlie Streeter. Over and over. He got on my nerves. Like I said, I was sure I was going to need the police."

"Then what happened?" Angie's eyes were like lasers on Brenda.

"Nothing. He finally gave up. He left."

"Did he give you his name? His number?"

"No. He didn't tell me his name."

Angie's shoulders slumped in disappointment. This man was a clue. A thought popped into her head. "Is there a security camera in the office?"

"The police took it. It probably wouldn't be of any help anyway. Half the time it wasn't working." Brenda narrowed her eyes. "Why so many questions about this guy? He showed up *after* Carlie and Marty were killed. If he was the killer, he'd know Carlie wasn't in the office. He'd know she was dead."

Angie forced a smile. "I was wondering why he wanted to see Carlie so badly. That's all."

It wasn't all. This man knew something ... and Angie needed to find out what it was.

15

The Roseland sisters and Mr. Finch had dinner at the Pirate's Den Restaurant in the center of Sweet Cove and then decided to stroll through town to get ice cream and do some window-shopping. Jack and Rufus had gone to Boston to see a client, Tom was working late on the new project he'd started, and Josh was in a late evening meeting with a banker. Mr. Finch's girlfriend, Betty, was showing a few houses to a family new-to-town.

The soft, warm air caressed their skin as the family walked along under the golden pools of light from the old-fashioned streetlamps. Tourists and townsfolk meandered over the brick sidewalks to the stores and restaurants and down to the beach to walk in the white sand beside the ocean.

Jenna strolled beside Angie. "I haven't seen the ghost of Jeremy Hodges again. Only that one time when he was in the backyard of the Victorian standing under the pergola. Sometimes I imagine he's in the room with me, but I think it's just my mind playing tricks on me."

"Why did he only show up once?" Angie asked as she took a lick of her ice cream.

"Maybe he moved on?" Jenna speculated. "Maybe he crossed over? He died a violent death. I've read that dying that way can cause a spirit to linger before being able to cross."

"He showed up in the backyard," Angie said. "He must have been looking for you."

"Why though?" Jenna thought over the possibilities. "Was he looking for help? I'm glad he hasn't shown up again. I wouldn't know what to do for him. I don't know the first thing about how to help someone cross."

"Well, he must have sensed you could see him so he came by." Angie poked her sister with her elbow and smiled. "Maybe you'll have a bunch of ghosts showing up from now on. They seem to know where you live."

Jenna let out a groan. "Well, they're sorely mistaken if they think I know what I'm doing. One of them should spread the word that Jenna Roseland is useless."

"Maybe they'll help you learn about them and what they need."

Jenna shook her head. "If I'm going to inherit these abilities and skills, could they at least come with an instruction manual?"

Angie let out a guffaw and Ellie, Courtney, and Mr. Finch turned around to see what she was chuckling over. When she explained what they'd been talking about, Ellie said, "Good grief, I agree with Jenna. If we had some instruction, things wouldn't seem so scary."

"Do your skills frighten you?" Courtney eyed her sister.

"Yes," Ellie practically shouted. "I'm afraid I won't be able to control it. What if we were at the restaurant and I wanted the salt shaker and just by thinking about it, the thing levitated and floated over to me." A look of horror washed over Ellie's face.

"Wouldn't that be cool?" Courtney smiled.

"No, it certainly wouldn't. People would talk about me and what I'd done. I'd become a freak. I'd get run out of town."

"You could always join the circus," Courtney kidded.

"So not knowing how to control your skills worries you, Miss Ellie?" Finch remarked. "That's why you never want to use them?"

"That's part of it, yes." Ellie's fair skin looked even paler than usual.

Angie was impressed that Ellie was being so forthcoming about her concerns. Whenever it came to paranormal powers, Ellie wanted nothing more than to run from them as fast as she could.

"You should talk to Cora," Angie suggested. "She might be able to help you feel more comfortable with your powers."

"Maybe." Ellie said the word so fast and clipped that Angie knew the discussion was now over.

Chief Martin and his wife, Lucille, came out the door of an Irish pub and they all greeted one another before walking together down the street.

"I talked Phillip into going out for a while," Lucille told them. "I thought it would do him good. He's so wrapped up in those murders, working day and night. This job takes an awful toll on him."

Angie didn't want to say anything to the chief about who she'd recently talked to and what she'd learned, thinking it could wait until the next day. Chief Martin needed a break and discussing the visit from the receptionist would only serve to drag the man back into a crime-solving mindset.

Despite her resolution not to bring up the murders, the chief sidled up beside Angie. "Talk to anyone today?" he asked quietly so Lucille wouldn't hear even though his wife was busy talking to Ellie about recipes.

Angie's eyebrow raised. "You aren't supposed to talk about such things right now."

"It doesn't matter if I talk about them or not. I'm always thinking about what's going on." The chief leaned closer and whispered. "Lucille thinks a night out gets my mind off things. It doesn't. I humor her."

Angie shook her head at the law enforcement officer and told him about what she'd learned from the receptionist.

"Huh," the chief said. "So the dentists fought a lot. Everything wasn't all peaches and cream. I'd give the notion more importance if one of the dentists was still alive. They couldn't have tied each other's hands and then stabbed one another. They didn't kill each other." The chief sighed. "A couple that doesn't get along can point to other problems though."

Angie said, "I found out one other thing." She told the chief about the man who came to the dental office the morning of the murders demanding to see Carlie. "Did the police take the security camera from the dentists' office?"

"They did. Nothing useful was found. The camera was terrible. There was some grainy film from the day before and then the whole thing goes snowy. It's been sent for enhancement, but they won't be able to do anything with that rotten piece of film."

"I need to find the guy who visited the dental office on the morning of the murders," Angie said. "I think he holds a clue of some kind."

"Might be like looking for a needle in a haystack." The chief eyed Angie's ice cream cone. "That sure looks good." After a few seconds, he returned his attention to the matter they were discussing. "I'll give the patrolmen the description of the guy, see if he's still around town."

"Is your team any closer to solving this thing?" Angie asked hopefully.

"Still investigating."

Angie knew that was the standard reply when there wasn't anything new on a case.

"I wondered if the lot of you would be willing to come back to the manor house. Walk around, see if you can pick up on anything we might be missing."

"We can do that. Well, most of us can."

"Ellie?"

Angie nodded.

"It's understandable" the chief said. "No need to make her uncomfortable. Let her stay at home." After a few moments, he asked, "What about the cats?"

"You want the cats to come?"

"If they don't mind." Even though he had no idea how the cats could do what they did, the chief knew the felines were able to sense things from both people and objects and he didn't think it would hurt if they visited the crime scene.

"What did you think of Tara Downey when you spoke with her?" Angie asked.

"She's forthcoming with information. She contacted the police when Jeremy didn't come home or answer her texts. She came right down here to talk to us." The chief turned his head to look at Angie as they walked. "Miss Downey is able to keep her emotions in check."

"I noticed that." Angie finished off her cone. "It's possible the couple was on the verge of breaking up and that's why she isn't very upset over Jeremy's death."

"Maybe she loves drama," the chief said. "I've

met people like that over the course of my many years of investigating crimes. Some people are attracted to the excitement of a sudden death, they like the attention they're receiving. I've been to training on grief. Grief can make people behave in odd ways, in ways other people take as inappropriate. It's not unusual behavior, it's just some folks' reaction to death. It doesn't mean they don't care."

"Hmmm." Angie thought about what the chief had told her. "I guess it makes sense. When I talked to Tara, she mentioned Jeremy's friend up in New Hampshire. Has anyone been up to see him?"

"Joe Winkler. I went up to talk to him. He didn't have a lot to say. He owns the auto body shop. He said he was busy. The guy seemed broken up about his pal."

"Did he talk about Jeremy and Tara's relationship?"

"He said they were a normal couple." The chief gave a shrug.

"He didn't know why Jeremy came down to Sweet Cove?" Angie asked.

"He said he had no idea."

"Not much help. Jeremy must have kept his plans to visit here a secret. Why would he?"

"The million-dollar question."

"And how did he get down here?" Angie asked. "Someone must have given him a ride."

"Still digging into that."

Lucille pointed out a man's jacket in the window of a shop and Chief Martin agreed to go in and try it on. Before he went into the store, he asked, "Would you and some of the others mind a little drive up to New Hampshire to talk to the auto body owner and maybe a few other people? Sometimes people clam up when a law enforcement officer asks them questions. You might have better luck getting some answers."

"We can do that, sure." Angie gave the man a smile. "See you tomorrow."

Chief Martin and Lucille wished everyone a goodnight and headed into the men's shop to take a look at the jacket.

Watching them go, a flood of anxiety flashed through Angie and she had the impulse to call out a warning to the chief, but she stifled herself not understanding what was bothering her. She pushed the urge aside and tried to analyze the worry.

Unable to figure it out, she let out a soft breath and followed after her family suddenly wanting the comfort of home.

16

Angie and Jenna got out of the car and walked across the parking area of the Top Shop Sales, Service, and Auto Body business. Cars in different states of repair were parked on one side of the lot, two Porsches, three BMWs, a Mercedes, and a Corvette. The blazing sun reflected off the hot metal of the autos practically blinding the sisters.

No one was behind the desk in the office, so they stepped through the open garage doors into the noisy work area of whirring drills, welders, and sanders and looked around for Joe Winkler.

A guy pulled off his protective eye-wear when he noticed them standing at the entrance and loped over to them. "Help ya?"

Jenna smiled at the man and introduced herself

and Angie. His name, *Joe*, was embroidered above the pocket of his shirt. Joe was tall and sturdily built with big shoulders and muscular arms. His dark blond hair was cut close to his head and he wore greasy jeans and a tight, blue, short-sleeved t-shirt. The beginnings of a beard covered his chin. Joe declined to shake hands due to the grease on his palms.

Jenna explained the reason for their visit. "We were friendly with a dentist who worked here in town and who moved to Massachusetts not too long ago. Her name is Carlie Streeter. Do you know who she is?"

When he heard the name, Joe seemed to stiffen. "I'd don't go to the dentist much."

Angie said, "Carlie died recently. We understand your friend Jeremy Hodges worked in Dr. Streeter's office for a couple of years. We're sorry about your friend's passing."

"Thanks." Joe ran his hand over his face. "Oh, yeah, that's right. Dr. Streeter. Yeah, Jeremy worked there."

"Would you mind talking with us?" Jenna asked. "We won't take much of your time. We're trying to figure out what happened to our friend."

Joe looked back at the car he was working on

obviously wanting to come up with an excuse not to chat with the young women. "Ah...."

"We promise not to stay long." Angie gave Joe a hopeful smile.

"I guess. There's a picnic table over there." Joe gestured to a scrappy area of grass where a broken down picnic table sat under a tree.

"You've got a busy place here," Angie noted. "A lot of high-end cars to work on."

"Everybody gets into accidents, all cars need work, expensive cars, old cars, everything in between. There's never a lack of business."

Sitting in the shade under the tree offered temperatures a few degrees cooler than out in the direct sun. Sweat beaded on Joe's forehead. He swiped at the drops with the back of his hand. "It's too hot. I like the winter."

Angie gave a nod. "Do you know why your friend, Jeremy, was in Sweet Cove?"

"I have no idea."

"Had he mentioned he might take a day trip?"

"Not to me."

Jenna pushed her long braid over her shoulder. "Was anything bothering Jeremy? Did he seem nervous about anything?"

"No. He seemed himself, far as I know."

"Was he upset when Dr. Streeter and Dr. Chase moved their dental practice to Massachusetts?"

"He didn't want to lose the job. He liked working there. He said the people were nice, easy to work with. He wasn't upset, he just felt bad about having to look for something else that he might not like as well."

"Did he consider moving to Massachusetts so he could keep his job?"

"He did, yeah. It's not that far away from here. His girlfriend wasn't keen on the idea of moving and commuting. He tried to change her mind, but it was a no go."

"That was Tara Downey?" Jenna asked.

Joe's eyebrow raised. "Yeah, Tara. She's a nurse. She didn't want to move. She liked where she was working."

"Was Jeremy angry about Tara not be willing to move for him?" Jenna asked.

"Oh yeah, he sure was." Joe caught himself. "It didn't last long though. Jeremy wanted to stay with Tara."

"Were they serious about each other? Do you think he and Tara would have gotten married some day?" Angie asked.

Joe shifted around. "I don't know. I don't know if Jeremy was ready for marriage."

"What's Tara like?" Angie asked the man.

"I don't know her very well." Joe shifted his gaze from Angie to Jenna. "She's okay."

"Did you hang out together sometimes?"

"With Tara and Jeremy? Nah, just Jeremy. Tara never seemed like she liked me much."

"Why not?" Jenna questioned.

"Maybe, jealous a little bit? I think she wanted Jeremy all to herself. She didn't like him going out at night without her, or me and him going fishing or whatever."

Angie tried a different question in order to get Joe to loosen up and talk more. "How did you meet Jeremy?"

A smile formed slowly over Joe's face. "I was at a bar. Some guy started hassling a girl. She was with a group of her friends. The guy was hanging all over her. The girl wanted to leave and headed for the door, but the guy grabbed her arm and pulled her back to him. I got...." Joe was about to swear, but changed the word he was going to use. "I got angry. The guy was a real jerk. The girl started to cry. I went over to them. Jeremy went over to them at the same time. I grabbed the guy by the back of his shirt and Jeremy took the girl by the arm and turned her away from the guy. The guy started to have a fit. Needless to say, Jeremy and I both got in a punch or two before he collapsed on the floor. Cops came. The girl told the police that me and Jeremy saved her from the guy. That was a little dramatic, but it got us off the hook. Me and Jeremy were good friends after that."

Angie smiled at the man. "Was that a long time ago?"

"Yeah." Joe looked off into the distance and sadness tugged at his face. "Almost ten years ago. I can't believe Jeremy is gone."

With a soft voice, Jenna asked, "Can you think of anyone who would want to hurt him?"

Joe turned and looked at the brown-haired young woman sitting across from him. "Jeremy was a good guy. He worked hard. People liked him."

"Could drugs have been involved?" Jenna asked. "Did Jeremy take any drugs?"

Joe let out a snort. "No way. That guy was as clean as a whistle. No drugs. He'd barely drink a beer. He told me once his parents had drug problems, were alcoholics. Jeremy was determined not to fall into that stuff."

Angie asked, "Did Jeremy keep in touch with Dr. Streeter and Dr. Chase after they moved?"

Joe sat straighter on the picnic bench. "I don't think so. He never said anything about it. I don't know for sure, though."

Angie thought of something else to bring up. "Jeremy's car was in the lot at the office where he worked. The staff saw it that morning ... the morning Jeremy died. How did he get to Sweet Cove if his car was here? Was there a friend he might have asked for a ride?"

"Got me." Joe shrugged. "He didn't hang around with anyone else that I know of. Jeremy worked, went home. He and Tara went out once in a while. I'd see him now and then. I don't know who could have given him a ride."

"Have you ever been to Sweet Cove?" Angie watched Joe's face.

"Me? Ah, I don't think so." A muscle twitched at Joe's jaw. "Maybe as a kid."

"It's a nice town," Jenna told him. "It's right on the ocean with really nice beaches. It has a great center with restaurants and shops, a village green. And only a mile from the center is Coveside which is right on an inlet cove with lots of boats docked there.

There are pubs and restaurants, nice shops. It's great. You should visit sometime."

"Sounds like a nice place." Joe glanced back to the garages.

Angie saw Joe look away and she didn't want him to finish the conversation. "What do you think happened to Jeremy?"

"I don't know what happened. Somebody killed him. He must have run into some nut."

"Why would he be at the dentists' house?"

Joe stared at Angie, but didn't say anything.

"Did he have some business with them? Was he visiting?"

Joe repeated what he'd said previously. "I don't know what happened. I don't know why he was at that house."

"Do you have any guesses?" Jenna asked. "Can you think of any reason he might have gone to Sweet Cove?"

Joe stood up. "I said I don't know. I have to get back to work now."

Angie hurried to her feet. "I'm sorry about Jeremy. Thank you for talking to us." She extended her hand. "I don't mind a little grease."

Joe hesitated, but then reluctantly took her hand and shook. He turned to Jenna and did the same, and then he strode away to the building where he fixed the cars.

When he was back inside, Jenna and Angie walked slowly to their car.

"What do you think?" Jenna asked her sister.

"I think Joe knows more about Jeremy than he's telling."

"Yeah. That's for sure." Jenna took a quick glance back to the garages. "What are we going to do about it?"

"I have no idea," Angie said.

17

Having the uncanny ability to transfer the emotions she experienced while baking into the dough or filling she was making, Angie was being careful not to think about the murder or the people she'd interviewed while mixing flour and sugar together in a big bowl. If she didn't control her feelings, then the person who ate the bakery item would feel the same emotions she'd had while making it.

"What's cookin?" With a bowl of ice cream in her hand, Courtney plopped into the seat at the kitchen island still wearing her candy shop apron. Euclid and Circe perked up from their perch on the refrigerator when they sniffed what Courtney was snacking on.

Without looking up, Angie said, "I'm making some muffins and cookies and a banana bread."

"Make extra. I'm hungry for sugary things today." Courtney licked her spoon. "I haven't see you since you went to New Hampshire to see the auto body guy."

"Joe Winkler."

"What happened up there?" Courtney dipped her spoon into the creamy chocolate chip ice cream with marshmallow topping.

Angie gave her youngest sister the summary of the trip north.

"Huh. He knows more about Jeremy than he's telling you. I bet he knows why Jeremy came to Sweet Cove."

"Why wouldn't he tell then?" Angie scooped the mixture from the bowl to the muffin tins.

"He's afraid," Courtney speculated. "He's worried that telling what he knows will get him into trouble. Or he's afraid that if he talks, he'll get someone else into trouble."

"Or ..." Ellie entered the room. She was wearing a tennis skirt and had her blond hair pulled up into a bun. "The man has been warned that if he tells why Jeremy came to Sweet Cove, then he'll end up dead, too."

Angie and Courtney looked at Ellie.

"You think someone threatened him?" Angie asked, her forehead scrunched with concern.

"I see this all the time on the crime shows I watch with Mr. Finch," Courtney said with excitement in her voice. "Somebody knows something and the person gets warned not to tell the important thing he or she knows. Then they either tell and end up dead or they don't tell and the police suspect *them* or the criminal doesn't get apprehended. At least not right away."

Angie said, "I don't know. Joe seems like a tough guy. I don't know if he'd let someone push him around."

Courtney savored the last of the ice cream. "If someone has a gun, Joe would probably do what that someone tells him to do."

Ellie filled her water bottle from the fridge. "If Joe has a loved one and that loved one was threatened, then I'd bet he'd do whatever he was told to do."

"You're right." Angie let out an angry sigh. "I wonder if Joe is married, or if he has a child."

"Chief Martin must know if Joe has family," Ellie said.

At the mention of Chief Martin, a flash of anxiety filled Angie's chest.

Courtney noticed the look on her face. "What's wrong with you?"

Euclid and Circe stared down at Angie.

Angie rubbed at the tension in her neck. "Ever since the other night, every time I see him or hear Chief Martin's name, I get a terrible feeling of anxiety."

"Oh, no." Ellie's eyes went wide and she stood still in the middle of the room.

"Do you feel anything specific about him?" Courtney asked.

"No." Angie shook her head as an expression of helplessness crept over her face. "Should I tell him what I'm feeling?"

"No." Ellie's voice was adamant. "What good would it do to tell him unless you have something specific for him to be on the lookout for?"

"I think Ellie's right." Courtney folded her arms on the countertop. "If you give the chief some vague warning, it might just make him so nervous that he won't be fully on guard. That could make things worse. We don't want to paralyze him so he isn't able to react to a threat."

"I guess you're both right," Angie said sadly.

"Whenever we're with him, we need to be alert to any danger. We need to be ready if anything happens."

"Nobody's taken us down yet, Sis." Courtney gave her sister a warm smile.

"And nobody will this time either." Ellie picked up the tennis racquet from the kitchen table where she'd left it and turned to her sisters. "I'm going to meet Jack. Nothing's going to happen to Chief Martin. You need me? You call or text right away."

"I will." Angie smiled at the fierce mother-bear instinct coming from Ellie.

The front doorbell rang and Ellie said she'd see who it was on her way out. In a minute, she was back. "Marty Chase's mother is here. She was looking for Mari Streeter, but Mari went out. Mrs. Chase asked for you," she told Angie.

Angie wiped her hands on a dish towel and after asking Courtney to watch the muffins in the oven, she followed Ellie to the foyer.

"Angie," Mrs. Chase smiled when she saw her. "I'm meeting Betty Hayes, the Realtor, in a little while. I stopped by to see Mari Streeter, but she's not here. We're putting Carlie and Marty's house on the market. Neither of us wants to keep it, so why wait. Do you have a minute?"

Angie and Mrs. Chase went to sit in the living room.

Mrs. Chase let her eyes wander over the furniture, the fireplace, the muted colors in the rug, and the artwork hanging on the walls. "What a lovely room. So beautiful and relaxing. Did you decorate it yourself?"

"It was pretty much like this when I inherited the house," Angie told her.

"Lucky you." Mrs. Chase wasn't smiling and there was a trace of jealousy in her tone that gave Angie a shiver. "I wonder where Mari went?"

"I don't know," Angie replied. "Did you ask Ellie?" Angie wished Mrs. Chase would get to the point of why she wanted to talk.

"I didn't, no." Mrs. Chase shifted a little on the sofa. "I saw your boyfriend driving around in that red antique roadster. He likes cars?"

"He does." Angie wondered how the woman knew Josh was her boyfriend.

"Marty loved cars, too." Mrs. Chase looked wistful. "It didn't matter what kind of car, he loved them all. He and Carlie had a few nice automobiles when they died. I have no use for them and neither does Mari. Would your boyfriend have any interest in any of the cars? There's a Lamborghini, and a Mercedes, and a Ferrari. Oh, and a Porsche."

"I don't think he would, but I can ask him." The blue Lamborghini could be a hard sell since a dead body had been found in it. She guessed Josh wouldn't be bothered by that fact. Maybe he could pick it up at a good price.

"Please do. I'd like to get this stuff off my hands as quickly as possible."

"Can you sell them to a dealer if no one wants them?" Angie asked.

Mrs. Chase said, "I think so, but like I mentioned, I'd like to offer the vehicles to people from your town first." The woman looked down at her hands. "Marty and his cars. He couldn't get enough of beautiful, fast cars. Carlie went along with his hobby."

"She liked cars, too?"

"Marty said she did." Mrs. Chase raised a shoulder. "I don't know if she really did or was just trying to keep Marty happy."

"Did the couple seem happy recently?"

Mrs. Chase met Angie's eyes. "Why would you ask?"

A ping of annoyance bounced in Angie's chest. "Because they were murdered. It makes me wonder what was going on with them."

"Nothing was going on," Mrs. Chase answered with a tone of irritation mixed with defensiveness. "Some crazy person decided to kill them."

Angie didn't think that was the case and she wondered what was behind Mrs. Chase's surety that the couple's activities, associations, or behaviors had no part in the event.

Angie knew she'd asked the question before, but she wanted to hear what Mrs. Chase would say this time, "Do you think Marty or Carlie might have known or been acquainted with the killer?"

"It's possible." Mrs. Chase sniffed. "But I don't think anyone who knew them would want them dead." She waved her hand around in the air. "Oh, sure, Marty could be abrasive, but was that enough to make someone kill him? And if someone was angry at Marty, why kill Carlie, too?"

"Had Marty ever mentioned Jeremy Hodges to you?"

"No, he didn't. I never heard the name. I don't know why that young man was on their property." Mrs. Chase let out a breath that sounded like a soft groan. "The police certainly have their work cut out for them."

"Had you ever heard the name Tara Downey?"

"No. Chief Martin told me she was Jeremy Hodges's girlfriend."

Angie gave a nod. She tried another name. "What about Joe Winkler?"

Mrs. Chase blinked at Angie. "Joe Winkler? What's he got to do with this?"

With her heart rate increasing, Angie said, "Mr. Winkler was a friend of Jeremy Hodges."

A tinge of pink colored Mrs. Chase's cheeks. "Was he? Well."

"You knew Mr. Winkler?"

"Me? Oh, no. I never met the man. Marty knew him from living in New Hampshire. He brought his cars to Winkler for service. He mentioned it to me once. He said the man knew his stuff ... he trusted him with his cars."

Angie's head started to pound as bits and pieces of information swirled around in her brain. Joe Winkler knew Jeremy *and* Marty. Jeremy had worked for Marty and Carlie. What did it mean? How did these connections relate to the murder?

More pieces of the puzzle had just fallen into her lap.

18

The night air was warm with only a mild trace of humidity as the family and their friends gathered in the garden for dinner. The torches had been lit and the flames danced under the starry sky. Strings of little white lights had been wound around the top and the posts of the pergola and jar candles on the wooden table glimmered beside the white plates and glass goblets.

Mr. Finch and Betty sat next to the fire pit with Chief Martin and Lucille enjoying drinks and appetizers. The two cats rested in the grass nearby watching Courtney, Rufus, Jenna, and Tom play badminton under the lights shining from the side of the carriage house. Ellie and Jack moved gently back and forth on the garden swing while Angie and Josh handled the grill.

Angie glanced over to Chief Martin and her now familiar flutter of unease rushed over her skin making her heart sink.

"Angie?" Josh held an ear of corn in his tongs waiting for his fiancée to hold the plate for him.

"Oh, sorry. I got distracted." She picked up the platter and Josh removed the corn from the grill. Angie set it down on the outside side table. "Have you given any thought to buying one of Marty Chase's cars?"

"It's tempting, but I don't want to spend the money right now." Josh leaned over and kissed Angie. "I have to save my money. I'm getting married."

Angie's eyes sparkled. "Oh, are you? Do I know the lucky girl?"

"You might." Josh grinned at his sweetheart. "She lives around here."

Angie's laugh glittered in the air.

Tom called from the badminton game. "Stop flirting with each other, you two. You'll burn the food."

Turning the conversation to a serious subject, Angie asked, "What do you think about this case? Jeremy Hodges worked for Marty and Carlie in New

Hampshire. Jeremy was friends with Joe Winkler, the guy who owned the auto place where Marty brought his cars for service."

"There are a few threads running between people." Josh turned the teriyaki chicken breasts.

Chief Martin heard what Angie and Josh were discussing. "Marty and Carlie were in financial trouble. Marty seems to have been the spender in the family and was burning through money like a madman."

Betty Hayes said, "That's why that poor woman came to see me about selling the house they'd recently purchased. She told me the property was much too big for them and that it was foolish to have bought it in the first place. She wanted to downsize, get a smaller place with a smaller yard."

"That's probably what they'd been fighting about," Angie said. "According to the dentists' receptionist, the fighting had gotten worse over the past weeks and the relationship between Carlie and Marty seemed very strained."

"He must have refused to put the house up for sale," Mr. Finch speculated.

"Marty must have known the money was disappearing faster than they brought it in," Josh said.

"Initially I wondered where they got all their money ... what with the big, fancy house and all the sports cars, but they had overextended themselves with their borrowing."

"The day of financial reckoning was probably close at hand." When Finch sipped from his glass of whiskey, the ice cubes tinkled when they bumped the sides of the tumbler.

"I think there was no avoiding bankruptcy." Chief Martin stood up and stretched. "And it would have happened very soon."

Rufus came over to the grill to offer assistance. "Smells wonderful." He picked up another platter so Josh could remove the meat and vegetable kebobs. "I sure wish I made enough money to buy one of those cars." Rufus made sure his voice was loud enough for Jack to hear.

Jack responded from the garden swing. "I heard that and you're not getting a raise."

Rufus lowered his voice. "If my employer was more generous, I'd buy Marty's Porsche in a second."

Something pinged in Angie's mind. "Have you seen that car lately? Marty and Carlie were in an accident in it. He drove it into a tree."

Rufus looked horrified that the beautiful car had been damaged. "Was it totaled?"

"I was just wondering that." Angie turned her attention to Chief Martin. "Do you know anything about the car?"

"I don't. Maybe Mrs. Chase knows what happened to it."

Rufus let out a groan as he carried a platter to the table. "If that was my car, I would have treated it like a baby."

Everyone took their seats and devoured the delicious teriyaki chicken, macaroni and cheese, corn on the cob, vegetable kebobs, baked potatoes, and tomato, onion, and cucumber salad. Strawberry shortcake with whipped cream was served for dessert.

After much laughter and chatter and tea and coffee were served, the group began to disperse promising to meet again in two weeks for game night at the Victorian.

Chief Martin gave the Roseland sisters a hug and Angie noticed that he was rubbing his stomach.

"I ate too much," the chief said. "As usual."

"He's had heartburn this week," Lucille told Angie. "He gets home late. He doesn't eat well when he's working on a hard case, even though I pack him a good lunch. He doesn't get enough rest. He eats a lot of fast food and junk, even with me harping on him."

"Harping on me means she loves me." Chief Martin smiled. "Tonight's meal was a real pleasure ... and the company even better."

The others left with goodbyes and hugs and Angie and Mr. Finch were the last ones left in the yard. The torches were out and the dishes had been carried inside, so they sat down near the fire pit, each with a cat in their lap, to watch the flames burn out.

"That Porsche," Angie said.

"I think so, too." Finch nodded.

Turning her head to the older man, she asked, "You think there's something about the Porsche?"

"I do. The doctors were in an accident. They walked away from the crash with bruises, whiplash, and minor cuts. Most likely, the vehicle was not totaled." Finch ran his hand over the top of his cane. "And it is certain the vehicle would need work. So where is it?"

A smile spread over Angie's face. "Top Shop Sales, Service, and Auto Body. Marty's mother told me he always brought his cars to Joe Winkler at Top Shop."

"You didn't notice a Porsche when you were there with Jenna?"

"I noticed two, but I don't know what Marty's car looked like," Angie said.

"Mr. Joe Winkler did not admit to knowing Dr. Streeter or Dr. Chase." Finch stroked his chin.

"He admitted to knowing that Jeremy worked for them." Angie adjusted her leg so that Euclid was spread more evenly over her lap. "But he didn't tell us that Marty always brought his cars to him. He also didn't say that he had one of Marty's cars, the Porsche, to work on right there, right then. Why didn't he?"

"Mr. Winkler doesn't want to acknowledge a connection to the man."

Angie asked, "Because Marty was murdered or for another reason?"

"That must be determined." Finch scratched Circe's cheek.

"It's a tangled web." Angie yawned.

"But the strands are starting to loosen."

"Do you want to take a trip to New Hampshire with me to visit an auto body shop one of these days?" Angie gave Finch a little smile. "Maybe we could talk to the owner."

"Even though it isn't far away, I have only been to

New Hampshire a few times. I would love to accompany you."

"Maybe we can get some more information out of Joe Winkler," Angie hoped.

"We will certainly try." Finch gently lifted Circe from his lap and placed her on the ground. "I believe I will head home now, Miss Angie. My bed is calling to me."

"I'm tired, too. I'll walk you home, Mr. Finch." She stood and took the man's arm and they strolled along the stone path from the Victorian's backyard to Finch's house with the two cats padding along behind.

"It was a very pleasant evening. We had a delicious meal," Finch said. "I'm ready to burst."

"Chief Martin said something similar." Angie's stomach clenched.

"We are all in agreement about the evening then."

"Do you feel anything?" A frown tugged at the corners of Angie's mouth.

Her tone of voice made Finch eye Angie. "About what in particular?"

"About Chief Martin."

Finch stopped walking and turned to face the young woman next to him. "Yes."

"What is it?" Angie whispered.

"I don't know. It started a few days ago. A sense that the chief is danger, but the sensation is vague and unformed. You feel the same thing?"

"Yes." Angie had to blink back a few tears. Thinking that danger was lurking nearby and would target the chief made her feel ill and helpless. "What should we do?"

"Be vigilant. Be ready. When whatever it is strikes, time will be of the essence. We will have to be quick."

"I talked to the others about what I feel. Courtney feels it, too. We don't think we should tell the chief our worries. It might make him so nervous that he misses whatever he needs to fight and then the danger gets the upper hand."

"I agree. Watching for it will make him more vulnerable. Nerves can interfere with the ability to act."

They started walking towards Finch's house again.

"Are you sure we shouldn't tell him?" Angie's voice was hesitant.

"I am sure." Finch nodded.

Tightening her grip on the man's arm, she said, "I don't like it, Mr. Finch."

"Whatever it is, it doesn't stand a chance against all of us, Miss Angie."

The cats trilled their agreement.

Despite Finch's and the cats' optimism, a sinking feeling tugged at Angie's heart.

But what if we all aren't there when he needs us?

19

When Angie, Jenna, and Mr. Finch emerged from the air-conditioned car into the late afternoon heat, Joe Winkler was standing outside one of the garage bays of his auto shop smoking a cigarette. When he spotted them approaching, Joe tossed the butt onto the ground, rubbed it out with the toe of his work boot, and shoved his hands into the back pockets of his jeans.

"We came back to talk," Angie told the man.

Joe's expression was cautious. "I thought you might." He took a glance at Mr. Finch. "You brought an associate?"

When Joe said the word *associate*, Angie knew he'd been the man at the resort asking about a meeting with his associate. "This is Mr. Finch, a family friend."

Finch extended his hand and Joe grasped it to shake, then gestured to the picnic table under the tree. "Shall we head to the office?"

Sitting in the shade out of the sun's hot glare, Angie asked, "Have you talked with the police again?"

"They paid a visit this morning." Joe's scruffy beginnings of a beard had started to fill in on his chin and cheeks.

Angie said, "You forgot to mention last time that you'd done business with Marty Chase."

"It must have slipped my mind." Joe rubbed his cheek.

"Did you talk about Marty with the police?" Jenna asked.

"We had a short conversation about him."

Mr. Finch had rested his cane against the table-top. "Would you be kind enough to tell us what you told them?"

Joe's tone was respectful, but firm. "I guess I have to ask why you want to know. What's your interest in all of this?"

"We're contracted consultants with the Sweet

Cove Police department," Jenna informed Joe. "We get called in on certain cases to interview people."

Joe's eyes widened in surprise. "The three of you?"

"Yes," Angie said. "There are actually five of us, but we work on different aspects of a case."

Several emotions flashed over Joe's face, confusion, disbelief, suspicion, and then near-acceptance.

"If you'd like to call Chief Martin in Sweet Cove to verify what we've told you, we don't mind waiting," Mr. Finch said with a nod.

Joe gave a resigned shrug. "It's okay. I don't need to call. What do you want to talk about?"

"Marty Chase. When we were here the other day, we asked if you knew Carlie Streeter. We neglected to ask if you knew Marty." Angie kept eye contact with Joe. "Our mistake. We need to ask some questions about Marty."

Jenna began. "What was Marty like?"

Joe seemed surprised to be asked about Marty's personality. "Marty was a decent guy. Loved cars. Was kind of obsessive about them. He enjoyed the glamour and flamboyant image they gave him. He could be a jerk, too, but that really didn't bother me. Marty liked to dress nice, tell everyone he was a doctor." Joe shrugged. "I didn't care. The guy had some need to show off ... so what? Some of the guys who work here didn't like Marty much. I say look for the good in the guy, leave the rest. Down deep, I think Marty was okay. Self-absorbed, yeah, but I don't think he was hateful or mean. He just had some need he had to fill."

Joe's analysis of Marty seemed dead on to Angie and she was impressed with his deep thinking about why Marty behaved as he had. "Marty brought his Porsche here to be fixed after the accident?"

"Yeah. It's over there. The police are going to bring it back to Massachusetts for examination."

"Why didn't you tell us this last time?" Jenna asked.

"I don't know you. Marty was a good customer. I thought he deserved some privacy."

"Even in death?" Finch asked.

Joe said firmly, "Yeah, even in death."

"Did you ever go out for drinks with Marty, go to a car show, anything like that? Did you spend time with him?" Jenna questioned.

"No." Joe's head moved from side to side. "It was strictly business. Oh, sure, we'd shoot the breeze for a while when he came up, but we weren't pals or anything."

"How did Marty seem the last time you saw him?" Angie asked.

Joe started to speak, then looked away to the patch of woods near the table, rubbing the back of his calloused hand over his eyes. He coughed. "Sorry. What the heck happened to him? Who'd do something like that to them? *Why* would they do it?"

"That's what we want to find out," Angie's expression was kind. "You can help us by telling us what you know."

Joe took a deep breath and didn't say anything for a few seconds before lifting his eyes to the people sitting across from him. "Marty seemed a little hyped up last time he was here."

"Hyped up, how?" Mr. Finch wasn't sure what Joe meant by the phrase.

"He had a lot of energy. He was talking really fast. He seemed to be sweating more than the weather would cause him to." Joe wore a serious expression. He was clearly making a point.

"Drugs?" Angie asked.

"I'm not sure. Marty seemed sort of manic. It could have just been his mental state. I've seen a few people on drugs. It could have been drugs causing his behavior. I don't know. I hadn't seen Marty like that before."

"Did you ask him if he was feeling okay?" Jenna leaned forward in a friendly manner.

"I did. I offered him some water, a soft drink, but he didn't want anything. He said he was fine. He said he had a lot on his mind. Marty always dressed nice. That day he looked a little disheveled. It wasn't like him. Looking good was important to him. His eyes were kind of glassy." Joe hesitated, and then said, "If I had to bet, I'd bet on drugs being the cause."

Angie told Joe, "Marty had some trouble with painkillers years ago. He'd been in an accident. He got addicted to the pain medication. Maybe he'd fallen back into needing drugs."

"I didn't know that. Marty always seemed really together, successful." Joe's face changed like something suddenly made sense to him.

Angie said, "I know we asked you before, but maybe you'd forgotten. Have you ever been to Sweet Cove?"

Joe looked at Angie shame-faced. "Yes, I have. And I didn't forget being there. I wasn't being truthful last time."

"When were you there?" Finch asked, although he knew what the answer would be.

"I was there the morning Marty and his wife got killed." Joe squeezed the bridge of his nose and closed his eyes momentarily. "I went back a couple days later, too."

Angie waited for Joe to continue. When he didn't, she asked him, "Why did you visit Sweet Cove?"

Joe swallowed hard. "Marty asked me to come down."

Eyebrows went up on the faces of the three people listening to Joe.

"Marty told me he was having some financial trouble. He said he couldn't go to a bank because he was overextended. He wanted to arrange a short-term loan from me. He asked me to come down to Massachusetts and meet him at a resort there. He said to ask at the desk for a Mr. Kravetz. He would rent a bungalow under that name so we could talk in private. He didn't want anyone to know about our meeting. Marty said the loan would be very short-term and that he would build in some very attractive incentives for me. He said it would be win-win for both of us."

"What happened when you got to the resort?" Finch asked.

"I arrived very early because Marty planned to go over the deal and then get back to the dental office. When I asked at the desk, the clerk told me there were no guests registered under that name. I got panicky."

"You thought something happened to Marty?" Jenna asked.

"No. Not at all. I thought I'd been set up somehow. That Marty was mocking me or something. I was pretty angry. I left and then decided to go to the dental practice to see what Marty was up to. I wanted to chew him out." Joe wiped sweat from his brow. "I looked up the address of the office. I parked and headed up the sidewalk. The closer I got to the place, the more I thought that something might be wrong. I couldn't think of a single reason Marty would invite me to a meeting on false pretenses. I had a bad feeling about it."

"You went in and asked for Carlie?" The receptionist told Angie that the man who showed up in the office after she and Courtney left that morning kept asking for Carlie.

"I went in and asked if the doctors were there. The receptionist said no. I got scared. I thought maybe Marty had been in an accident. I asked to talk to Carlie. The woman got annoyed with me and said Dr. Streeter wasn't in. I wondered if the woman was yanking my chain because I was being so persistent. There were patients in the waiting room. I thought one of the dentists had to be there. I kept asking about them and the receptionist got more and more agitated with me. I was afraid she'd call the police so I left. I went home." Joe's face seemed to pale. "Later ... I heard that Marty and his wife had been murdered."

Angie's heart clenched when she saw the look of anguish on Joe's face. No one said anything for a full minute.

Joe took a deep breath. "I thought about whether I should return to the resort and talk to the desk clerk. I decided to go to the resort again. I wanted to ask the clerk if someone else besides me came in that morning asking for a Mr. Kravetz or a Mr. Chase. I wondered if someone got to Marty before I arrived." Joe's jaw set. "I wanted to know who it was."

Angie realized that when she'd been on Robin's Point with Josh and Jack looking over the land plans, it must have been Joe she'd sensed at the resort. "What did the clerk say?"

"He said no one else came looking for either man that morning." Joe's shoulders slumped. "On the drive home, I panicked. I was afraid there was a security camera at the resort's front desk. What if the police thought I was the killer? I nearly drove off the road. Then when the police came up to talk to me ...

and then you came right afterwards, I was sure I was a suspect. I didn't know what to do. I clammed up."

"Did you go to Marty's house the morning of the murder?" Angie asked.

"No, I didn't. I did look him up on my phone trying to find his address. Nothing came up except the dental office's address so I went there." Anxiety etched into Joe's forehead. "Thank the powers that be that I didn't go to their house. I could have ended up dead. Or I might have found the bodies." Joe looked like he might faint.

"Did you see, run into, or meet with Jeremy Hodges that morning in Sweet Cove?" Jenna asked.

"I did not. I didn't know Jeremy was in town that day. I had no idea." Joe shook his head slowly and sadly. "If I had run into him, maybe he wouldn't have been at the manor house when the killer was there. Maybe he'd still be alive."

"Do you have any idea why Jeremy was at Dr. Chase's and Dr. Streeter's house that morning?" Finch watched the man's expression.

"I can't think of any reason. None at all. I'm sorry."

No one could think of anything more to ask Joe so they thanked him for his time and got up to leave. Mr. Finch fumbled with his cane and it fell to the ground. Joe picked it up and handed it to the older man. For several seconds, Finch and Joe held onto the cane at the same time.

Jenna took Finch's arm, and the three of them headed to the car.

When Joe was out of earshot, Angie asked Mr. Finch, "Did you sense anything when you and Joe held the cane?"

"Yes," Finch said quietly. "Mr. Winkler told us many things that are truthful, but he might not be telling us everything."

"Then he stays on the suspect list," Jenna said.

20

In the late afternoon light, Angie and Jenna walked along the sidewalks of town to the Streeter-Chase Dental Office. Chief Martin suggested that they visit with a hygienist who was in the closed office cleaning out her things. Emma Johnson had worked for Marty and Carlie in New Hampshire and moved down to Sweet Cove when the dentists relocated their practice to Massachusetts. The chief hoped that Emma would be more open in discussing the couple if some of the Roselands talked with her.

The shades were drawn on all the windows and there was a small sign on the door indicating that the office was permanently closed.

Jenna put her hand to the glass to knock and hesitated. "It's odd, isn't it? You and Courtney were here only a few days ago. Now everything has changed." With a sigh, she gave a knock on the door.

After a few minutes, footsteps could be heard and a hand moved the shade away so the young woman could take a peek out. When she unlocked the door, she asked, "Angie and Jenna? Come in. I'm Emma." Emma, in her twenties, was short and petite, with short black hair, perfect skin, and blazing white teeth. Angie had no idea how someone could possibly have such white teeth. She guessed working in a dental office provided Emma with products that turned her teeth to alabaster. Angie couldn't help staring at them.

The waiting room and reception area were dark and the emptiness gave the space a gloomy atmosphere.

"I'm working in back." Emma led the way to a cream-colored room that seemed to be a place for the employees to store their things, eat lunch, and have their breaks. A large table sat in the center with six chairs around it and two sofas had been placed in a corner near the windows. Some boxes had been stacked on the floor near a wall of closets. "I'm taking all the stuff out of the closets and setting them aside for people to come pick up their stuff." Emma gestured to the chairs and they sat down.

"Chief Martin told me you were crime consultants and asked if I would talk with you. I don't know how I can help. I don't want to waste your time."

"It's never a waste to talk," Angie reassured the woman. "Things that seem inconsequential often turn out to be important and can end up helping to solve the crime."

Emma didn't look convinced.

"You worked with the dentists in New Hampshire?" Jenna asked.

"I did. Dr. Marty and Dr. Carlie were good to work for. That's why I moved down here with them. I was ready for a change and thought moving would be a nice adventure." Emma frowned. "Not the kind of adventure I was planning on."

"Are you moving back to New Hampshire?" Angie asked.

"I'm not sure. I have a six-month lease here in town. If I can find work, I'll probably stay."

"How long did you work for the dentists?" Angie watched Emma pick at the corner of her fingernail.

"Um, about six years? Five and a half years were in New Hampshire."

Angie smiled encouragingly. "What was the office like? How were the doctors to work with?"

"It was a great office. Most people had been with

the doctors for years. People were nice. There was stress, but it was like we were all in it together. It was a really wonderful team." Emma's face began to crumble and she stopped talking until she managed to collect herself. "Sorry. I liked Dr. Marty and Dr. Carlie." Taking a tissue from her pocket, Emma dabbed at her eyes. "I won't ever find a better place to work."

Waiting until Emma had a chance to steady her emotions, Angie asked, "What did you think of Marty?"

Emma said, "He could be difficult, but he knew what he wanted done and if you followed his directions, you got along fine. It was like Dr. Marty was the complete opposite of Dr. Carlie. He was kind of full of himself, Carlie was humble and kind. Marty was quick and sort of boisterous while Carlie was quieter and calm. Marty was always rushing around, Carlie always had time to talk. They balanced each other out."

"Did you notice if things were getting tense between them lately?" Angie asked.

Something flashed over Emma's face. "Tense? How do you mean?"

"Did they argue a lot? Did they seem short with each other?"

"Marty and Carlie worked and lived together. I feel like they handled it all better than other people would be able to."

"Did you ever hear them arguing?" Angie tried again.

"Once in a while."

"Did they argue more in the last weeks of their lives?"

"I didn't notice."

Angie knew the woman was lying. "We understand how hard it is to answer questions about people who you liked. In cases like these, it seems wrong to talk about the people who have passed in anything other than glowing terms. When someone loses his or her life in this way, it's not unusual for people to want to rally around the person who died as if trying to protect or help him." Angie paused for effect. "If you really want to help Marty and Carlie, it's important to be honest and upfront with us."

Emma took in a short, quick breath and then nodded. "I don't want to tarnish their relationship by saying something dumb."

"You won't. No one is perfect. It's okay to speak about them as they were."

Emma looked down at the tabletop. "They were arguing more. I overheard their fighting pretty often.

It could be awkward. I'd be in here taking a break and they'd be in the room next door fighting about something. Most of the time, I couldn't hear their words. It was the tone of voice they used with one another. It was like they hated each other at the end."

"Did you have a sense of what they fought over?" Jenna asked.

"Money was a hot topic," Emma told them. "I heard Carlie tell Marty he had ruined them financially. She resented him for messing up their lives. They'd worked so hard and they had nothing but debt to show for it. They'd never be able to recover. That's what she said to him. I heard her."

"You worked in the New Hampshire office," Angie noted. "You must have known Jeremy Hodges."

Emma's big brown eyes got misty. "Sure, I knew him. He was a great guy. He was good at his job. The patients loved him. Jeremy was such a nice person, fun to be around. I tried to convince him to move down here when Carlie and Marty decided to relocate. He wanted to, but his girlfriend refused."

"His girlfriend was Tara Downey?" Jenna asked.

"Yeah." Emma's face changed when Jenna mentioned Tara.

"Had you met Tara?" Angie asked.

"A few times at parties Marty and Carlie put on for the office."

"Did you like her?" From the look on Emma's face, Angie thought she knew what Emma would say.

"She was okay."

"Did you think Tara and Jeremy were a good match?" Angie pressed.

"No." Emma let out a long breath. "He was great. She was sour and angry and jealous."

"What makes you say that?"

"Tara seemed really controlling. Jeremy and I got along great. Tara seemed jealous of our office friendship. I'm engaged. I wasn't looking for a boyfriend or a hookup. Jeremy and I never hung out together after work. I love my fiancé. Tara didn't trust me or Jeremy. At the office parties, she'd always be quiet around me, but she'd shoot daggers out of her eyes at me like she was giving me a warning or something." Emma looked about to say something else, but she hesitated, bit her lower lip, and changed her mind.

Jenna spotted Emma's reluctance. "Did Tara have any reason for jealousy? Did Jeremy ever meet up with other women? Did he ever cheat on Tara?"

Emma blinked a few times. "I don't think so. It would've surprised me if he did anything like that. He sure didn't tell me anything about seeing other girls. I think maybe Tara was just a jealous person. Maybe a boyfriend cheated on her in the past and she couldn't trust anyone anymore."

"Did you know Jeremy was in town the day he died?" Angie asked.

"I didn't know he was in Sweet Cove. I wished he'd dropped by here. I would have loved to see him." Emma's eyes glistened again with a few tears.

"Do you have any idea why he was in town?"

Emma shook her head. "I don't know. We didn't keep in touch."

"Do you think he maybe was asking the doctors for his job back?" Jenna asked. "Could that be why he was at their house?"

"Why would he go to the house?" Emma asked. "Why wouldn't he meet them at the dental office? If he wanted to work for them again, why wouldn't they meet at the office?"

"Was there an opening for a dental hygienist?" Angie asked.

"Not that I know of. If there was, I didn't know anything about it. There were three of us working. I didn't think the practice needed another hygienist."

Jenna said, "Maybe Jeremy was unhappy working where he was. Maybe he wanted to come back to Carlie and Marty's practice. He might have just shown up to ask about an opening."

"Maybe."

Angie sensed something wasn't being said. "From what we've heard, Jeremy loved working with Marty and Carlie. Is that right? Would you agree?"

"Yes, I would."

"He would have moved here if not for Tara's refusal?" Angie asked.

"I'm sure he would have."

"Maybe he changed Tara's mind."

"I doubt it. Tara didn't like Marty or Carlie."

"Why not?"

"Well, maybe she liked Marty, but she didn't like Carlie. That was clear from how she acted at those parties."

Unease ran through Angie's veins. "How did she act?"

"Like she did with me. Quiet, but giving us the evil eye."

"Out of jealousy?" Jenna asked.

"Tara didn't have to worry about me and Jeremy. She didn't have to worry about Carlie either."

"What *did* she have to worry about?" Jenna questioned.

Emma looked from Jenna to Angie. "Jeremy."

Angie and Jenna waited.

"Jeremy loved Carlie. He never said so to me, but there was no way to deny it."

"Carlie knew this? Did she reciprocate the feelings?" The tiny blond hairs stood up on Angie's arms.

"Gosh, no. Carlie knew Jeremy was in love with her. He was like a fawning puppy around her. But she had no feelings like that for Jeremy. It made her uncomfortable."

"How do you know how she felt?"

Emma said softly, "She told me."

Jenna thought she saw movement in the dark hallway and when she turned her head to look, she saw the translucent spirit of Jeremy Hodges standing just outside the door.

One tear spilled from his eye and traced slowly down his cheek. And then, he was gone.

21

Chief Martin asked Angie, Jenna, and Mr. Finch to return to Top Shop Auto Body to watch the Porsche being loaded onto a flatbed truck for return to Sweet Cove. Standing beside the automobile, neither one felt anything more than the arguing between Carlie and Marty as they rode in the vehicle before hitting the tree.

Since they were in Miltonville anyway, they decided to stop by Tara Downey's apartment to have a talk with her. It was late afternoon and they thought it was worth the chance to see if she had finished work for the day and was at home.

When they pulled in at the address Chief Martin had texted to them, they were surprised how nice the complex was. Brick townhouses were situated on the lots for maximum privacy and the area was well-landscaped with ornamental trees, flowers, and freshly mowed lush, green grass.

"This place seems very expensive." Jenna maneuvered the car into a visitor's parking spot.

"I wasn't expecting such a high-end place." Angie glanced around at the quiet, peaceful property.

After ringing the bell twice without a response from inside the townhouse, they decided that Tara must be out and turned to head back to the car when someone came around from the back of the next house.

"Are you looking for Tara? Can I help you?" A thirty-something auburn-haired woman walked over to them with a little white dog on a leash.

Angie introduced themselves and explained that they were consultants with a Massachusetts police department.

"You must be investigating the murder of Tara's boyfriend. I'm Lizzie Potter. I live next to Tara." She smiled. "We share a wall between our places."

"We didn't have an appointment," Jenna explained. "We were in town for something else and decided to stop by hoping Tara might be home."

"She's been out all day." Lizzie let the dog sniff around at some bushes. "In fact, Tara's been away from home a lot. I haven't seen much of her lately.

When I've run into her, she's been hauling stuff out of her place. I wonder if she's moving."

"Did you ask her if she was moving out?"

"I did, but she said she had to think it over before making a decision. I wondered if she didn't want to say anything about moving elsewhere. Why would she be moving stuff out if she hadn't made a decision?"

"Cleaning out clutter or things she doesn't want?" Jenna suggested.

"Her place was never cluttered. Tara's a neatnik. Everything is in its place. You could eat your dinner off of Tara's floor. She puts me to shame."

"Did you know Jeremy?" Mr. Finch questioned.

"Sure. The four of us had gotten together a few times for drinks in each other's places. We were friendly, not best buddies or anything. We'd run into each other and chat. My husband and I were shocked when we heard what happened to Jeremy." Lizzie shook her head. "So sad."

"Did you notice if Jeremy seemed like something was bothering him lately?" Angie asked.

"I didn't really see him enough to answer that question." Lizzie shifted around from foot to foot. "Tara and Jeremy didn't seem to be getting along lately."

Angie cocked her head. "What makes you think so?"

"We could hear some terrific fights going on next door. Not physical fighting as far as we could tell, but some real shouting and angry words. We thought we might have to call the police one night."

"Was that unusual?" Jenna asked.

"Yeah, it was. It had been going on for a couple of weeks though. I was pretty sure Jeremy would be getting kicked out one of these days."

Mr. Finch leaned on his cane. "How long have you lived here in the townhouse?"

"Just over a year."

Jenna asked, "Why did you say Jeremy might be getting kicked out?"

"The place was in Tara's name. She told me once she was sorry she hadn't told Jeremy he had to pay half the living costs. Tara paid for the place herself." Lizzie smiled. "My husband got a different story from Jeremy. Jeremy told him that he'd offered to pay half for the townhouse, but Tara refused. She gave me the impression that she didn't want any help from a guy or didn't want to be beholden to anyone. Tara was super independent. Is the crime close to being solved?" Lizzie asked.

"We don't have that information," Jenna said.

"We interview people and pass our findings to the investigators. The police don't share details with us."

"Oh." Lizzie's face looked sad. "I hoped someone would be arrested soon for Jeremy's murder. He was such a nice guy, very thoughtful, kind. I ran into him one day when we were bringing trash out. My mom had died. She'd been an alcoholic my whole life. I was upset. Jeremy talked to me. He said his parents had problems with drugs and alcohol. He was very sympathetic and caring." Lizzie reached down to pat her dog. "I can't believe what happened to him. Such a waste."

"Before the last couple of weeks, did Tara and Jeremy seem close?" Angie asked.

"I guess so. Tara was never demonstrative, not in front of us, anyway. We didn't see them together a lot. Tara seemed like the boss of the relationship. She was kind of stand-offish, she wasn't a real warm and fuzzy kind of person, but once you got her talking, she was nice. She seemed like she had lots of friends. People used to stop by all the time. I got the feeling Tara didn't trust many people. She seemed careful. Who knows what she's been through in life, and now this. Poor woman."

"Tara works days?" Angie asked.

"Her schedule changed from time to time. Sometimes she worked days, other times she worked nights."

"Do you know what her schedule is this week?" Jenna asked.

"I don't. I'm not sure, but I think she took some time off from her job. It's understandable. When she comes home, she usually only stays for a bit and then takes off right away."

"Have you talked to her since Jeremy's death?"

"Not much. I made a lasagna for her right after we heard what happened. She wasn't home much and we couldn't deliver it to her so we ate it ourselves. She doesn't seem to want much acknowledgment of what happened from other people. I'm sure she's feeling emotional and is afraid to break down if she talks about it."

"When was the last time you saw Tara?" Angie asked.

"Oh, gee. I don't know." Lizzie thought it over. "At least three days ago?"

"Maybe we'll stop by the hospital where she works and see if she's almost done for the day." Angie thanked Lizzie for talking with them and they started to walk back to the parking lot. Glancing over her shoulder, she watched Lizzie and her dog go inside to her townhouse. "I'd like to take a look around Tara and Jeremy's property, have a look around the yard. If we can, maybe take a peek in some of the windows, but I don't want any neighbors to see us snooping around. We can't stay long. I don't want Lizzie to catch us poking around Tara's place."

"What are we looking for?" Jenna asked.

"I don't know." Angie led them the long way around so Lizzie wouldn't see them from her window. "I got a funny feeling when we were talking to the neighbor. I don't know why or what it means."

The three walked through the landscaped flowerbed on the far side of the townhouse's property so no one would see them traipsing through the yard. They headed for the back deck. There was a high fence between the decks that separated Tara and Jeremy's home from Lizzie's.

Quietly, they went up the steps and took a look in a few of the windows.

Angie stood straight, her face serious. "Well, so much for being able to eat from Tara's floor."

Finch, Jenna, and Angie stared at one another.

In the kitchen of the townhouse, two chairs had been knocked over and spread across the counters and the floor were shards of broken dishes, cups, a frying pan, and ... a knife.

"There isn't any sign of blood that I can see,"

Finch said. "Perhaps Ms. Tara was packing things and they fell out and broke."

Nervousness gripped Angie's stomach. "I hope that's all it is."

Jenna pulled out her phone. "I guess we'd better contact Chief Martin."

Angie's brain swirled with questions. *What happened in there? Where's Tara?*

22

Jenna called Chief Martin and reported what looked like it might be the scene of a fight or of an intruder in Tara Downey's kitchen. After he contacted the Miltonville, New Hampshire's law enforcement department, Chief Martin said he would drive up to the townhouse to inspect the place and confer with the officers of Miltonville.

Angie, Jenna, and Mr. Finch planned to head to the hospital where Tara worked to see if she was there or to inquire if anyone she worked with knew where she was.

The hospital consisted of several attached three-story, gray-shingled structures built in the New England Cape Cod style. Shade trees, flower borders, and flowering bushes gave the place a peaceful, comfortable feeling. Chief Martin had shared that Tara worked in the cardiac unit of the hospital so the three amateur investigators headed to the nurse's station on that floor.

When Angie stepped onto the grounds, she'd experienced moments of vertigo and on entering the hospital, the dizziness increased. Feelings of weakness and exhaustion flooded her body and the words of Mari Streeter talking about the physics of time, time travel, the Big Bang, and parallel universes kept replaying in her mind. *Time, seconds.* Angie's heart pounded hard and she almost felt like she was going crazy.

Approaching the medical staff's desk, Jenna said, "Sorry to interrupt. We're looking for Tara Downey and wondered if she might be working today." She went on to explain their connection with the Sweet Cove police and offered a number for them to call to verify what she was saying.

"Tara has taken a few days of personal time." The nurse behind the desk told them.

"Do you know if she went away? Did she go to stay with someone?"

"I don't know. She might have. I didn't hear her plans. Did you try her townhouse?"

"We did." Jenna gave a nod. "Is there anyone on

staff that Tara was friendly with? Someone who might be in contact with her during her days of leave?"

"Maybe Lynn Bolton. She isn't working this shift. She'll be in for the 11pm to 7am shift, if you'd like to come back."

"Would it be possible to get her contact information?" Jenna asked even though she knew it was a long shot.

"I'm sorry. We aren't allowed to give out that information."

Continuing to feel oddly, Angie stood to the side listening. She'd hoped that her weird sensations would disappear, or at least wane, but they remained steady and strong. She had the unusual urge to cry and she had to think about pleasant things to try and distract herself from her feelings of anxiety.

Leaving the hospital, they stepped out into the late afternoon warmth.

"What should we do?" Jenna asked.

"Why don't we have a seat on the bench over there in the shade and discuss." Mr. Finch used his cane to point to two park benches set in a small garden off the entrance to the medical facility.

"Are you feeling okay, Miss Angie?" Finch asked after they'd sat down.

"I'm tired I guess. I feel sort of weak. I might be getting a headache." Angie's face was pale and her facial muscles looked tight.

"Why don't we go home?" Jenna looked at her twin sister with concern.

"No," Angie's voice was loud and strong. "No, I can't." She didn't have any idea why she said she couldn't go home. She rubbed her forehead to try and release the tension built up under the skin.

Finch and Jenna exchanged worried looks.

"Why don't we go get a cold drink or a snack somewhere," Jenna suggested. "We can sit in a café in the air-conditioning and take a break."

Angie agreed and as they were about to leave the bench, a woman, in her fifties, skinny, with bleached blond hair came up to them.

The woman seemed hesitant to speak and her eyes flicked between the two sisters and Finch. "Um, hi. I work in the hospital. I heard you asking for Tara."

Mr. Finch smiled, stood, and introduced himself. "Would you like to sit with us?"

"No, I ... I just wanted to talk to you for a minute. If you have time."

"We do," Finch said kindly. "We'd be happy to speak with you."

"I don't want to give you my name." The blonde looked over her shoulder back to the hospital entrance. "I'm a nurse's aide. I've been working here for forever. I don't want to get anyone into trouble. I don't want to lose my job."

"We can keep what you say in confidence from the hospital," Finch said. "We may have to report what you tell us, but we don't have to report *who* told us. We can keep your identity in confidence."

The woman seemed to relax a little. "Okay, thanks."

"Why don't you sit?" Finch gestured to the next bench.

"I've worked on all floors and units, but I've been in cardiac for about a year." The blond nervously tugged at the hem of her shirt. "I know Tara."

"What can you tell us?" Jenna asked gently.

The woman sucked in a breath. "I've been worried about Tara. She was kind of forgetful lately. She made a mistake on a patient that I caught. It was a mistake with medication. She was angry that I told her she was doing the wrong thing, but I think she was secretly thankful that I kept her from making a big mistake."

"Has she become forgetful since her boyfriend died?" Jenna asked.

"It was before that. I noticed changes in Tara about a month before he died."

"What sort of changes?" Finch sat straight holding his cane between his knees.

"Tara was really forgetful. She seemed kind of distracted. Some days, she didn't have much energy. Other days, she was really witchy and mean."

"This was out of character?" Jenna questioned. "She didn't act like that before a month ago?"

"Tara wasn't that easy to work with. She was demanding. She could be quick. Sometimes she didn't act that friendly. She was really smart and good at her job. This past month though, she was like a different person, like she was new and inexperienced. It seemed like her mind was somewhere else. I like her. I'm worried about what's going on with her."

"Tara took some time off?"

"She did. I think it was the smartest thing to do. You can't work in a hospital and make mistakes. It could end a career."

"Did Tara go away? Did she go to stay with someone?"

"I didn't hear anything about that. I thought she was at home, but that might be wrong." The woman took a look back to the entrance. "I need to get back to work. I hope Tara's okay." She stood to go. "If you see Tara, tell her I hope she comes back soon. Well, tell her *someone* at the hospital hopes she comes back soon. Don't let her know I talked to you." She turned and headed quickly back inside.

Jenna and Mr. Finch discussed the conversation they'd had with the hospital worker and when Jenna noticed that Angie didn't have anything to say, she took a look at her sister. "Angie?"

"Huh? Sorry. I feel like a zombie. I must be coming down with something. I feel like it will take all of my energy to walk back to the car." Angie's phone buzzed in her bag and she dug it out to read the text. "It's Chief Martin. He's at Tara's townhouse. He wants us to come meet him there."

"Maybe we should go home." Jenna was concerned about Angie.

"Let's go see him, and then we can go home." Angie dragged herself from the bench and plodded towards the car, her legs feeling like heavy blocks of cement.

～

ANGIE AND MR. FINCH held onto one another's arms as they followed Jenna up the walkway to Tara's townhouse. Two police cars were parked in the driveway. Chief Martin's personal car was parked at the curb. As the group from Sweet Cove entered the home, two officers who were heading out gave them a nod.

Chief Martin was in the living room and when he saw Angie, his eyes went wide. "What's wrong with you?"

"I think I'm coming down with a bad cold." Angie's heart felt like it was racing and the dizzy feeling had returned. She sank onto the living room sofa glancing around the room at the mess. A chair had been overturned, books from a wall of shelves had been knocked to the floor, and papers were scattered over the rug near a desk.

"What a mess." Jenna looked around.

"Is every room like this?" Finch walked around the space to have a closer look. "Is there any sign of a break-in?"

"None. Someone might have come to the house and Tara knew him. She might have let him in. Maybe the person got aggressive and Tara took off." Chief Martin removed a notebook from his pocket. "An upstairs room has been ransacked and so has the dining room. It might be a robbery, but we don't know if anything's missing until Tara comes home."

"Any sign of blood?" Jenna looked down the hallway to the kitchen.

"Just a few drops in the bathroom sink. Probably from someone getting cut on the broken dishes." The chief wrote some notes his small book.

"A woman at the hospital talked to us," Angie managed to tell the chief. "She'd worked with Tara. She told us Tara had been acting oddly, being forgetful, making mistakes she'd never have made in the past."

They discussed other things the woman had told them.

Chief Martin stroked his chin for a moment. "What was bothering Tara Downey two weeks before her boyfriend got killed?"

No one had an answer.

Jenna suggested they head home and despite a few complaints from Angie, they got up and said goodbye to the chief.

"Thanks for coming up here." The chief gave a nod. "You found out useful information. It's a big help."

"Are you leaving now?" Angie asked weakly.

"Not for a little while. The Miltonville Chief of Police, George Hannaford, has gone to pick up some sandwiches for us. He and I will go over what we know and try to tie some things together."

"Good luck with it all," Jenna told him.

Jenna, Mr. Finch, and Angie left the house and walked towards the car. When they got in, Angie collapsed in back, rested her head against the top of the seat, and closed her eyes. Despite her exhausted state, information rushed through her mind and wouldn't allow her to doze as the car sped along. The words she'd heard Dr. Mari Streeter say kept ricocheting around in her head. *Time. Seconds.*

Angie broke into a sweat. A few miles from Tara Downey's townhouse, Angie fell into a fitful sleep, but in less than three minutes, she woke and sat bolt upright.

"Go back. Go back." Angie was frantic. "Turn around. Hurry."

As Jenna wheeled the car around and floored it, Angie yanked her phone from her bag and dialed "911" to send an ambulance and the police to Tara's address.

With her heart pounding in her ears, words swirled in Angie's brain. *Seconds, seconds. Hurry.*

She knew.

23

Jenna screeched to a halt at the curb in front of Tara Downey's townhouse. Chief Martin's vehicle was still parked on the side of the street.

"Something's going to happen to the chief," Angie had told Mr. Finch and Jenna on the drive back. "I don't know what it is, but he's in trouble."

Ellie had texted Angie as their car approached the townhouse asking if they were all okay because the cats were acting crazy, running through the Victorian and howling.

All three piled out of the car and stared, in the darkness, at the house.

"I sense something as well," Mr. Finch said quietly. "Nothing has happened to Chief Martin yet, but something terrible is floating on the air."

"What should we do?" Jenna took Angie's and Finch's arms. "Should we wait for the police to arrive?"

"It will be too late if we wait." Angie started up the front walk.

"Hold on." Jenna went around to the back of her car and popped the trunk. When she closed it, she had a tire iron in her hands. She looked at her sister. "Now let's go."

"We need to hurry." As they made their way to the front door, Angie looked over her shoulder to the street. "Where are the police and that ambulance?"

"Since the chief is still safe, maybe we don't need the ambulance." Jenna hurried along behind Angie and Finch.

"We'll need it," Angie muttered. "Let's go around back to the kitchen."

Walking quietly and gingerly up to the deck, Angie could see Chief Martin's back and another man standing a few yards from him. A person stood in front of both men.

With a lunge, the person rushed at the other man and then moved back a few steps as the man staggered and fell. The chief bent to assist him.

It was a woman who was in the room with the

men. She darted towards the kneeling chief just as Angie grabbed the doorknob and pulled. Locked!

"Chief Martin!" Angie turned to Jenna and shrieked. "Break the glass!"

Jenna moved forward with the tire iron and bashed the glass to pieces. Reaching in through the broken window, she unlocked the door and swung it open.

The chief had crumpled to the floor and Tara Downey was running from the kitchen.

As Jenna went after Tara, Angie rushed to Chief Martin's side. He had lost consciousness. Angie searched his chest and limbs for knife wounds. Nothing. Glancing at the other man unconscious on the floor next to the chief, she crawled to him and checked him for wounds. Again, there were no signs of knife wounds. She checked the man's neck for a pulse and felt a faint beating.

Mr. Finch dropped his cane, knelt beside the chief, checked for a pulse, and began chest compressions.

Tears poured down Angie's face. "Chief, Chief." She knew they only had seconds to save him. Swiveling on her knees, she began compressions on the other man's chest. *Seconds, seconds. Stupid ambulance. Get here!*

Sweat poured off of Angie and Finch. Mr. Finch sat back. "I need a few seconds rest."

Angie swiveled on her knees and started compressions on the chief. She whispered, "Don't you die. Don't you leave us."

Finch reached for Chief Martin's neck and checked again for a pulse. His face paled and he looked to Angie with tears in his eyes.

"No, no, no." Angie wouldn't stop pumping.

As Finch began to work on the other man, the scream of the ambulance's siren bounced off the walls. Within a minute, a man and a woman dressed in uniforms rushed through the open door, their feet crunching on the broken shards of glass.

"What happened?" the woman demanded.

The man set down a medical bag.

Angie slid back on her butt a few feet from the chief so the paramedics could step in.

"We don't know." Angie's head was spinning. She closed her eyes and the image of Jeremy Hodges's dead body sprang into her mind.

Shaking, Angie pushed herself to her feet. "Narcan! Give them narcan!"

The two paramedics stared at Angie for a second and then went to work injecting the two fallen men with the opioid antidote and doing CPR on the chief.

In less than three minutes, Chief Martin's eyes fluttered open and closed ... opened and closed.

"Just in time," the woman paramedic said to no one in particular.

Seeing the chief come back to them, Angie's heart did a flip of joy and then a horrified look washed over her face. "Jenna."

Angie ran into the hallway calling for her sister.

When two police officers burst through the open back door, Finch told them what had happened and urged them after Jenna and Angie.

Running through the dark townhouse, Angie kept calling. The basement door was open. Angie stopped short. Terrible moans could be heard coming from the cellar. "Jenna?" she asked softly.

"I'm down here, Angie. Put the light on."

Angie flicked the wall switch to light up the basement and darted down the staircase to see Jenna holding the tire iron and standing over the crying and moaning Tara Downey. "I might have broken her leg."

Angie couldn't help it when she said with disgust, "Good."

Jenna held Angie's eyes with a look of dread and asked the question she wasn't sure she wanted to hear the answer to. "The chief?"

The two police officers tore down the steps with their weapons drawn as Angie wrapped her arms around her twin. "Chief Martin is alive."

"Just in time." Jenna smiled. "We got here just in time."

It only took a second for tears to spill from their eyes, trace along their cheeks, and drop onto each other's shoulders. The sisters held one another in a bear hug, their hearts beating close and strong.

24

Tara Downey was arrested for the murders of her boyfriend, Jeremy Hodges, Dr. Carlie Streeter, and Dr. Marty Chase. Tara found out that Jeremy was in love with Carlie by discovering a separate phone in his dresser. A few weeks before he was killed, Jeremy had used the phone to send emails and texts to Dr. Streeter asking for his job back and telling her that he planned to leave Tara and move to Sweet Cove.

There was only one email from Carlie explaining to Jeremy that it wasn't a good idea for him to move and that there weren't any openings at the new dental office. Tara was sure there must be more correspondence from Carlie and that Jeremy must have deleted the other emails. Having been cheated on twice in the past, finding out that Jeremy wanted to leave her for Carlie Streeter pushed Tara over the edge.

Tara reported to the police that she used her position at the hospital to access drugs and then she concocted a cocktail of opioids which she used to inject Jeremy with while he was sleeping. With great difficulty, she'd dragged her boyfriend's dead body from the bed to her car in the garage and drove, early in the morning to Sweet Cove, with the intention of dropping the body on Dr. Streeter's front steps.

Before leaving for Massachusetts, Tara's anger reached explosive levels and she decided to kill Carlie, too, so she packed a hunting knife and more of the powerful drugs. To confuse the police, Tara moved Jeremy's car to the place he worked to make it seem he was still alive that morning.

When she rang the dentists' bell early that morning, Marty answered, and recognizing Tara, he opened the door and escorted her to the kitchen so he, Tara, and Carlie could talk.

Before they reached the kitchen, Tara swiped the knife across Marty's throat. Carlie heard the commotion, saw what happened, wheeled, and ran trying to escape through the back door, but Tara was quick.

Carlie was killed in the same way that her husband was.

To make it look like a robbery gone wrong, Tara bound the couple's hands after they were dead. She found the key to the blue sports car and stuffed Jeremy's body into the tiny trunk hoping that blame for his death would fall on Dr. Streeter and Dr. Chase.

There was a pond on the dentists' property behind the house. Tara went into the water, clothes and all, to get rid of the blood spatter. If she was stopped by police on the way back to New Hampshire, she planned to tell them she'd fallen into a pond while taking early morning photographs and did not have a change of clothing.

Tara believed that Chief Martin was getting close to discovering that she was the murderer so she obtained more drugs to put an end to the man's life. Tara admitted to rampaging through her house in a fury over Jeremy's attempted infidelity on the very day Angie, Jenna, and Mr. Finch came to talk to her. When she saw the three people coming to her door, Tara went out the back and up the hill to hide in the wooded area between the townhouses and the town park.

When she saw Chief Martin and the Miltonville Police Chief together in her townhouse, she was sure they were about to arrest her. She snuck into her house, went to her bedroom for the syringe of drugs, and attacked Chief Martin and the other law enforcement officer by injecting the opioids into their systems. Tara would most likely have additional charges filed against her for the attempted murder of Chief Martin and Chief Hannaford.

"And so that's what happened," Jenna finished telling the group about Tara Downey's crimes.

"Ms. Downey is being evaluated at the psychiatric hospital near her town," Finch reported. "A very sad tale."

Chief Martin had spent some time in the hospital and had been recently discharged to the care of his loving wife, Lucille. The Roselands and Mr. Finch had been bringing home-cooked meals and bakery goodies to the Martins almost every evening and Euclid and Circe visited along with them, taking turns curling up on the chief's lap.

The chief was getting stronger by the day and Lucille told the family that the enforced rest and relaxation was having a beneficial effect on her husband. The chief, of course, was chomping at the bit to get back to work.

The morning after the attack on the chief, all four Roseland sisters and Mr. Finch visited their dear friend in the hospital and when they gathered around his bed, there wasn't a dry eye in the room. During the first few minutes of the visit, nobody was able to converse because emotion had choked each one of them.

With tears streaming down her face, Angie gripped the chief's hand in hers and held it to her heart. "Don't ever do that again," she whispered.

Chief Martin's cheeks were wet with his own tears. "I'm not crying," he insisted, which caused everyone to laugh and then things went back to normal with the six of them happily chattering away.

On the way out to the car after the visit, Mr. Finch, walking between Angie and Jenna, said, "Sometimes we don't realize how much we love someone until we almost lose them."

The sisters hugged the older man and Angie slipped her arm through his as they all crossed the parking lot to their car.

Finch said, "Dr. Mari said something strange to me the other day."

"What was that?" Courtney asked.

"When she heard about our rescue of Chief Martin, she brought up time travel again."

"Did she?" Ellie eyed Mr. Finch.

"What did she tell you?" Jenna asked.

Finch said, "Dr. Mari suggested that perhaps we had the ability to travel through time."

Ellie gasped.

"She said maybe we had previously experienced what had happened to the chief, then went back in time to live through the event again, but with the knowledge gained from the first experience to save the chief from death."

Courtney cocked her head. "So the first time, Tara's injection killed Chief Martin? Then we went back in time so we could save him? That was why we felt that he was in danger? Because we'd already lived through the experience?"

"That was her suggestion," Finch nodded.

"That's a load of you-know-what," Angie's voice was forceful. "We didn't time travel. That is crazy talk. All we did was sense danger."

"And being able to sense danger is less crazy than time travel?" Courtney laughed.

"Wouldn't we know if we time-traveled?" Jenna asked.

"What did you say to Mari when she mentioned this to you?" Ellie asked.

Finch winked. "I told Dr. Mari that we had many

wonderful skills, but time travel was not among them."

The four sisters all chuckled and agreed whole-heartedly with Mr. Finch. Just before climbing into Ellie's van, Jenna noticed something out of the corner of her eye. When she turned her head, she saw the ghost of Jeremy Hodges standing several yards away. Jeremy made eye contact with Jenna, nodded to her with his hand over his heart in a gesture of thanks, and then he slowly disappeared.

WITH THE SUN lowering on the horizon, Josh and Angie, Jenna and Tom, Ellie and Jack, and Courtney and Rufus, along with Mr. Finch and Betty, and Mel and Orla sat in beach chairs in a circle on the white sand of Sweet Cove beach. Angie, Jenna, and Mr. Finch took turns finishing the tale of the gruesome murders and the attack on Chief Martin committed by Tara Downey.

"Thankfully," Finch said. "Both chiefs of police are recovering nicely."

"How did you know to turn around and call the ambulance?" Rufus gave Angie a look.

"It was my intuition that kicked in." Angie

shrugged her shoulders. "It's a good thing I listened to it."

"That's for sure," Rufus agreed. "A few seconds made all the difference. You arrived in the nick of time ... and so did the paramedics. Otherwise...." Rufus didn't finish the thought.

"Enough of all this." Josh stood up. "Let's get the dinner going."

Ellie had parked her van along the street next to the sidewalk that followed the curve of the shoreline so they could easily access the food and supplies they'd packed into the vehicle. The young people unloaded the car and Josh and Tom used small shovels to dig into the sand to make a fire pit. They placed charcoal in the hole and set a large wire grate over the flames that soon started. Chicken, burgers, corn on the cob, and baked potatoes were placed on the grate to cook. Coolers of drinks were carried down to the chairs.

Finch, Betty, Mel, and Orla made gin and tonics, pushed their toes under the warm sand, and watched the others run down to the water and jump into the waves.

"Would you like to swim, Mr. Finch?" Mel asked.

"I'm quite happy here in my chair with a towel over my legs as I enjoy the sea air and sip my drink." Finch raised his glass, clinked it against Mel's, and winked. "I believe that being young is overrated."

"I'll drink to that." Mel let out a hearty laugh.

Betty and Orla brought over a platter of crackers and cheese, passed it around to the men, and then placed it on one the small tables Josh had set up next to the chairs.

"What a beautiful evening," Orla said with a wide smile on her face. "I wouldn't want to be anywhere else or with anyone else." Thinking about Finch's actions when he was at Tara Downey's house, the woman looked kindly at the older man. "You are a brave man, Victor Finch."

"Oh, no, I'm really not, Ms. Orla." Finch swirled the liquid in his glass. "I only sprang into action because I didn't want to lose anyone who is dear to us. I must admit that when I couldn't find Chief Martin's pulse, I almost lost hope."

"Never lose hope, Victor," Orla told the man. "And call us in as reinforcements, if you ever need to. We'll always lend a hand."

The young people chased each other at the edge of the ocean and bodysurfed in the waves.

Angie splashed sea water at Josh and he ran after her along the sand until he grabbed her into a hug, pushed the wet hair from her cheek, and kissed her under the pink, violet, and sapphire sky.

"I'm proud of you," Josh told his fiancée. "You use your skills to bring the bad guys to justice, to bring some comfort to victims' families. You make the world a better place." Looking into Angie's eyes, he added, "Just please remember to use your skills to keep *yourself* safe. I'm not sure what I'd do without you, Angie Roseland."

On that warm summer evening, Angie reached up to kiss Josh and then they walked hand and hand back to check on the dinner cooking on the grill, feeling happy to be with their family and friends, and oh so lucky to have each other.

THANK YOU FOR READING! RECIPES BELOW!

Books by J.A. WHITING can be found here:

www.amazon.com/author/jawhiting

To hear about new books and book sales, please sign up for my mailing list at:

www.jawhitingbooks.com

Your email will never be sold, shared, or spammed.

If you enjoyed the book, please consider leaving a review. A few words are all that's needed. It would be very much appreciated.

BOOKS/SERIES BY J. A. WHITING

*CLAIRE ROLLINS COZY MYSTERY SERIES

*PAXTON PARK COZY MYSTERIES

*LIN COFFIN COZY MYSTERY SERIES

*SWEET COVE COZY MYSTERY SERIES

*OLIVIA MILLER MYSTERY-THRILLER SERIES
(not cozy)

ABOUT THE AUTHOR

J.A. Whiting lives with her family in New England. Whiting loves reading and writing mystery stories.

Visit me at:

www.jawhitingbooks.com/

www.facebook.com/jawhitingauthor

www.amazon.com/author/jawhiting

SOME RECIPES FROM THE SWEET COVE SERIES

CREAM CHEESE AND LEMON MUFFINS

INGREDIENTS

MUFFIN BATTER

1 cup all-purpose flour

1 teaspoon baking powder

¼ teaspoon baking powder

⅛ teaspoon salt

4 ounces cream cheese (may use regular or light); soften to room temperature

2 tablespoons butter, soften it to room temperature

¾ cup granulated sugar

zest of 2 large lemons

1 large egg

¾ teaspoon vanilla

¼ cup buttermilk

¼ cup fresh lemon juice

CRUMB TOPPING

¾ cup all-purpose flour

1½ tablespoons granulated sugar

2 tablespoon brown sugar

4 tablespoons butter, melted

LEMON GLAZE

3-5 tablespoons fresh lemon juice

½ cup powdered sugar

DIRECTIONS

BATTER

Preheat the oven to 350 degrees F.

Line a standard muffin tin (12 muffin size) with paper liners.

In a medium bowl, combine flour, baking powder, baking soda, salt.

In another bowl, with a handheld mixer or with a mixer fitted with a paddle attachment, beat the cream cheese, butter, sugar, and lemon zest together until light and fluffy.

Add egg, vanilla, buttermilk, and lemon juice; mix until well-combined; scrape the sides of the bowl.

Add the dry ingredients to the batter; mix by hand with a wooden spoon or a spatula until just combined. It is okay if the batter is a little lumpy.

Divide the batter between the muffin cups; fill cups about ⅔ full.

CRUMB TOPPING

Use the same bowl that held the dry ingredients for the muffin batter, whisk together flour, sugar, and brown sugar.

Add the melted butter and stir with a fork until mixture forms tiny clumps.

Top the muffins with the crumb topping.

GLAZE

Add lemon juice to a small bowl.

Whisk in powdered sugar, stirring constantly until well-mixed.

TO BAKE

Bake the muffins for 15-19 minutes or until a toothpick inserted in the center comes out clean.

Allow muffins to cool for 4-5 minutes; remove them to a cooling rack to finish cooling.

Finish the muffins with the lemon-sugar glaze.

74202185R10163

Made in the USA
Columbia, SC
26 July 2017